KT-482-168

SPANISH TYCOON'S CONVENIENT BRIDE

SPANISH TYCOON'S CONVENIENT BRIDE

NINA SINGH

MILLS & BOON

First published in Great Britain 2020
by Mills & Boon, an imprint of HarperCollins*Publishers*
1 London Bridge Street, London, SE1 9GF

Large Print edition 2020

© 2020 Nilay Nina Singh

ISBN: 978-0-263-08923-3

MIX
Paper from
responsible sources
FSC™ C007454

This book is produced from independently certified FSC™ paper to ensure responsible forest management. For more information visit www.harpercollins.co.uk/green.

Printed and bound in Great Britain
by CPI Group (UK) Ltd, Croydon, CR0 4YY

To my own family,
I love you all more than words can say.

CHAPTER ONE

SHE REFUSED TO look at the picture yet again. What was the point? There was really no use in torturing herself every single day. The image of her and Carlos grinning at the photo booth camera as she sat in his lap was now nothing more than a harbinger of pain.

When he'd finally answered his phone after weeks of not hearing from him, his reaction was exactly what she'd been afraid it would be. His words from their last phone call echoed through her head.

Not ready...caught by surprise...one day perhaps...forgive me...

Ha! Cassandra Wells turned over onto her back where she lay on her twin-size mattress and stared at the swirly paint designs on her ceiling. As if she'd be able to forgive him anytime soon. Or ever. Though she would have to find a way to get over it all, wouldn't she? Because she'd be connected to Carlos Alhambra forever now. Carlos, the man who'd courted her, enticed her and then left her with nothing but useless, empty words.

Carrying his child.

She should just burn the stupid photo. That would eradicate the urge to look at it over and over again, hoping to find something that would shed light on how she could have so badly misread the man she'd fallen head over heels in love with over the course of a few days.

A nagging inner voice poked at that thought, telling her perhaps she'd been more in love with the concept of being in love. Look where it had gotten her. Pregnant and alone. A predicament she swore she'd never find herself in given the way she'd been brought up.

Cassie sighed and counted slowly until the churning in her empty stomach could subside. Then she slowly rose to make some breakfast and start preparing for her day. No doubt, it would be another tiring one. That seemed to be her state of being these days—exhausted and constantly on the verge of tears.

She knew it must be the hormones, but that didn't make dealing with all the emotional turmoil any easier. She'd always considered herself something of a loner. But this was the first time she felt utterly, completely alone.

Her hand instinctively reached for her midriff and she rubbed it affectionately. Technically she wasn't alone at all. And she refused to see this child as anything less than the true gift that he or she was. Unlike Cassandra herself, her child would never feel the burden of feeling unwanted.

She just wished she had somebody to share the gift with.

Also, Cassie wished she was a better judge of character. How could she have been so naive? She'd foolishly indulged in a frivolous affair with a jet-setting Lothario with nary a thought to the consequences. Then it had taken days to contact him once she'd found out she was pregnant. Only to have him completely, utterly reject her and their baby once he finally returned her call.

Cassie's eyes stung and she forced them shut and blew out several deep breaths. No more. This was it.

She would not wallow in pity. She would not allow herself to stress out and jeopardize her and her baby's health. She could do it on her own.

It had been the story of her life, after all. She'd gotten through high school on her own. She'd seen herself through college with a major in hospitality studies. And she'd managed to find a rewarding, exciting job in a trendy metropolitan city like Boston.

A job that was becoming increasingly taxing as the weeks went by. But that was another story.

She could do this.

She just had to keep reminding herself. The first step was to forget Carlos Alhambra even existed. Because for her, he no longer did. Standing with determination, she walked over to the dresser where she'd tossed the damn picture after staring at it for the umpteenth time.

It would be the final time. Without another thought, hands trembling, she tore it in half. Then she kept tearing until it resembled tiny bits of confetti, their once smiling faces on the flimsy paper now nothing more than shreds.

That felt a little better. But it wasn't enough.

Even in a pile of small pieces, Carlos's slanted, boyish smile was still somehow visible. As was her foolishly trusting expression. She wanted to pretend the picture had never existed. She wanted to pretend that Carlos himself never existed. She wanted to somehow burn the past. Literally burn it. Walking over to the shallow porcelain sink, she dropped the bits of paper in the basin and then used a step stool to reach the book of matches she kept in a cabinet above the stove. Lighting two sticks at once, she tossed them into the sink. A small flame slowly emerged, and finally Cassie felt a small measure of satisfaction. Her friend Zara was a practicing Wiccan who spoke often of the power of fire and the performance of rituals using various earthly elements. Cassie hadn't given any of it much credence or even thought until this moment.

Zara would be proud of her.

Her friend was right. Watching the small pile of paper burn in her sink felt cathartic and freeing. The scent of smoke lent yet another sensory layer, as if the very air around her was cleansing.

Cassie spread her palm across her stomach and watched the flame grow larger and larger, the paper slowly curling and browning as it was consumed. Once the pile was nothing more than a heap of smoldering ash, she turned on the faucet.

She would have to call Zara later and tell her about the mini ritual she'd just performed. Closing her eyes, Cassie inhaled deeply the slightly smoky aroma that still hovered in the air. Peace. For the first time in several weeks, Cassie finally felt some semblance of peace.

It didn't last. An unexpected knock on her door made her jump and her eyelids flew open.

Who could be here to see her at this hour? And why hadn't the doorman buzzed in to alert her?

Grabbing a dish towel off the counter, she dried her hands and tossed it away haphazardly. Then went to see who her unexpected visitor might be.

She'd never been a fan of surprises.

It had taken him close to two hours to fight traffic and then find the right building. Julian

Santigo drove up to the adjacent parking lot of the high-rise and tried to clamp down on his frustration. But it wasn't easy. As tight as his schedule was on this trip, and as much as he had on his mind with the negotiations involved, he really didn't have the time nor the patience to be running some kind of fool's errand for the man he'd always thought of as a cousin.

Sometimes Julian wondered if he and Mama overindulged the man who was more like a relative to him than a lifelong friend. Even Julian's two younger brothers had been known to coddle their informally adopted kin. Carlos's misfortune of having been orphaned at a young age had weighed heavily on the Santigo family. Julian's mother had taken the boy in and cared for him as if he was blood.

As did Julian. Which was why he was here, in the newly developed Seaport District of Boston, after having had to navigate busy Boston traffic and road construction. Did it ever end? Julian wondered. It seemed every time he found himself in this city, there were massive construction crews exasperating an already terrible commute through the congested streets.

Julian parked the rented silver Mercedes and got out, grabbing the envelope he'd been asked to deliver on Carlos's behalf. Best to just get this over with, whatever it was. Carlos hadn't offered much in the way of explanation, was just adamant that the envelope be delivered personally by Julian since he was traveling to the Boston area anyway. He wanted to make sure the receiver accepted and, if possible, that Julian make note of her reaction. Julian had been too distracted to ask for details—Carlos had literally barged into his office in the middle of a high-stakes international conference call to make his request. Though *demand* might be a more appropriate word for it. And studying his surroundings now, Julian wondered if not asking Carlos for specifics might have been a mistake.

This was clearly a residential building, so it seemed unlikely that this was some kind of business transaction. Not that Carlos was much of a businessman in any case. He was much too busy partying his way across the globe.

Julian sighed and made his way toward the entrance of the building just as a sharply dressed woman in high heels and a curve-hugging wrap dress approached from the side. She didn't exactly hide the fact that she was studying him from head to toe. She seemed to like what she saw.

"Are you a new resident?" she asked as they both reached the door.

He shook his head. "Just here to visit someone."

The woman used a key card to swipe at a door slot and the latch opened with a buzzing sound. "Pity," she said, as she allowed him through first. "I believe I would have enjoyed having you as a neighbor."

Julian gave her a polite smile. He was used to this kind of attention in the States. Many American women seemed to have a "type"—dark hair and dark eyes with olive skin.

"Mr. Tall, Dark and Handsome," the woman added, confirming his suspicions.

He wasn't sure how to respond to that, he never really did when this happened on his visits to America. *Thank you* didn't seem quite appropriate. So he stayed silent as they both boarded the elevator.

The blonde spoke again. "Four-one-seven."

"I beg your pardon?"

"That's my apartment number. In case you're looking for something to do after your visit. I happen to be free *all afternoon*." Julian didn't miss the exaggerated emphasis on the last two words.

"Maybe next time." Not that he wasn't tempted. She was definitely attractive. And it had been a while since he'd enjoyed a pleasurable, no-strings-attached afternoon in the company of a beautiful lady.

The woman simply shrugged as the elevator doors opened for her stop. She gave him another alluring smile as she left. Julian watched her walk out with a suggestive sway of her hips. It couldn't hurt to make note of her unit number.

Three floors later, he exited himself and patted the inside pocket of his suit jacket. The sooner he delivered this mysterious document, the sooner he could be on his way. Walking down the hallway, he found the door matching the number Carlos had written on the envelope and knocked. Then he waited.

Several beats passed before Julian knocked again. It appeared there was no one home. That was actually a welcome surprise. He could simply drop off Carlos's delivery and be on his way. No such luck. He was getting ready to slide the envelope under the door when it opened slightly ajar. A set of chocolate brown eyes peered at him through the small opening. Then they blinked as if doing a double take.

"Yes?"

Suddenly, Julian felt foolish and out of place. Quite uncharacteristically, he hadn't thought this through. He was off his game. What exactly was he supposed to do here? Hand her the package and then click his heels and leave?

"Um… I have something for a Miss Cassandra Wells. Some documents."

"What kind of documents? Who are you?"

Again, he felt rather stupid. He'd simply been too distracted with his business concerns to give any of this much thought. "I'm not quite certain. They're from my cous—"

But he didn't get a chance to finish his sentence. Suddenly, the earsplitting sound of a loud alarm rang through the air. An acrid scent reached his nose just as a curtain of smoke wafted out the doorway.

"Damn it!" the woman shouted and disappeared from behind the door.

Julian sucked in a breath and swore silently in Spanish. Pushing the door open, he ran inside the apartment.

Carlos had literally led him to a fire.

She'd thought she'd doused out all the flames. Cassie ran back to her kitchen, the stranger at the doorway momentarily forgotten. Though her unexpected visitor was the reason for this mess. If there hadn't been a knock on her door, she would have never thrown that towel absentmindedly over the sink, where apparently it had caught fire. And it had spread. A pot holder sitting nearby on the counter had caught fire as well and had fallen to the floor.

She knew she had to act, but stood frozen. Maybe it was the hormones, maybe it was sheer protective instinct to not go near an open flame when she was carrying a child. But her feet were rooted where she stood.

Suddenly, a set of firm hands grabbed her by the shoulders and half lifted her off the ground to move her out of the way. The door knocker.

He reached over the flames in the sink to turn the faucet on. The fire went out with a hiss. Then he stomped on the pot holder until the flames on the floor extinguished.

The stranger from her doorway was yelling at her. "*Dios mio!* Do you have an extinguisher? To make certain it's all out!"

Cassie shook her head and blinked. The authority in his voice and the urgency of the situation finally broke her out of her stupor. Rushing to the pantry, she grabbed the fire extinguisher she kept on the top shelf. She'd barely reached the stranger's side when he forcefully grabbed the extinguisher out of her hands. In seconds, he had the hose out and angled to her sink, pouring white foam out onto the smoke. He did the same to the smoldering rag on the floor.

The alarm continued to sound, a jarring, pitchy noise that made her ears ring.

Time seemed to stand still but it appeared all the flames had finally gone out. Cassie could only stare at the mess that used to be her kitchen. A thin mist of smoke curled through the air. She felt the stinging behind her eyes and the churning in her stomach and willed them both to somehow subside. She so didn't need this right now. Not any of it. Though heaven knew she should be grateful. Things could have been so much worse.

And who was the stranger now standing in her kitchen? She still had no clue. For an insane moment when she'd peered through the peephole after his knock, she'd thought Carlos was standing at her door. There were many physical similarities. They certainly sounded alike. But she'd realized quickly it wasn't her former lover. This man had a hardness about him, a stern quality that she'd be hard-pressed to describe.

She'd always thought of herself as someone capable, a fighter. But she'd been utterly helpless just now during a full-blown emergency. In fact, she was a little alarmed at her reaction in the face of danger.

The stranger was breathing heavily, still brandishing the extinguisher in his hands when he turned to her. She opened her mouth to thank him for his quick thinking when his words stopped her.

He yelled at her over the bleeping alarm. "Are you always this careless, senorita?"

Twenty minutes later, Cassie walked out into the hallway with her apartment building's head of maintenance. He'd surmised that the sprinklers hadn't gone off because they'd contained the fire fairly quickly, but assured her he would be back to check they were in complete working order. Then he teased her about being a bad cook before telling her he was glad she was okay.

She returned to her living room, where Julian sat waiting for her. She'd only learned his name when he'd introduced himself to the maintenance staff after they'd come rushing in. She still had no idea who he was and supposed she still owed him a thank-you. Though it chafed a little that he'd accused her of being careless earlier. If that moment hadn't been so fraught, she might have given him a piece of her mind just then. He didn't know her, or what she was dealing with. And she still had no idea what he was doing here.

It was time to finally find out.

He sat leaning back against her cushions, and he looked completely out of place on her flowery, dainty sofa. A disquieting feeling nudged at her, as if she'd invited a predator of some sort into her own environment. And she was the prey.

Cassie shuddered and took a deep breath before she began. "Look, I'm really glad you were here to help me out. And I am grateful." She paused to make sure that statement landed. "But who exactly are you? Why are you here?"

He studied her before replying, "You're not even going to offer me a glass of water after all that?"

Cassie gritted her teeth, annoyed. Partly because he was right. She should have thought to offer him something.

She pasted a phony smile on her face. No need to be combative. He had just saved her from potential burns, after all. "Of course. I could use a drink myself."

In moments, she was back and seated across from him, pouring two tall glasses of water from a glass pitcher she always kept in the fridge.

Julian accepted the glass from her and took a long drink. Then he pulled an envelope out of his breast pocket and handed it to her.

"What's this?"

"Some paperwork I was asked to deliver to you."

"What kind of paperwork?" Was she being subpoenaed or something? Though the man sitting across from her looked nothing like a courier. Even in his disheveled state after putting out a fire, he looked none the worse for wear. His dark hair appeared only partly mussed and framed an elegant face with nearly black eyes. His well-tailored suit had nary a wrinkle and fit him like it must have been custom made. His almost imperceptible accent lent an air of intrigue and mystery whenever he spoke. Spanish, if she'd have to guess. Though Carlos's accent had been much thicker…

As soon as Cassie had the thought, the full reality hit her. She felt the blood rush out of her face and her heart slammed in her chest. Carlos had mentioned that he would make sure she was *taken care of financially*. She remembered responding with some rather colorful words of dismissal. If he wanted nothing to do with his child, she wanted nothing at all to do with him. He must have ignored her refusal of a monetary offer and sent some sort of compensation.

With all the panic of a live fire in her apartment, she hadn't been able to think straight and put it all together. Julian's next words confirmed what she'd already figured out.

"I'm not certain. I'm delivering them as a favor for my cousin, Carlos."

She'd gone visibly pale. Alarmingly so.

She stood abruptly with so much force that she nearly knocked the pitcher of ice water over. The woman really was a walking disaster. Demolition level. Exactly how klutzy was she?

"Is something wrong?"

She flung the envelope back at him without

looking at it. "You better believe something is wrong. Tell your cousin I want nothing to do with him."

Uh-oh. What had he walked into here? Whatever Carlos had meant to this Cassandra, they clearly had not left on the best of terms.

He cleared his throat. "Don't you want to know what's inside?" Suddenly, he was quite curious himself.

She shook her head. "Absolutely not. I don't want anything from that man. He's done quite enough."

She walked over to the door and held it open for him. "Now, I don't mean to be rude. But I'd like you to leave please. I've got quite a bit of cleaning to do."

Just like that. She wasn't even going to ask him any more questions.

Julian knew his cousin to be quite a ladies' man. And some of those ladies often became pretty angry in the aftermath of his affairs. But this particular woman seemed to be different. There was more than anger at play here. Below the fury, Julian could sense a layer of hurt. She exuded a hint of vulnerability underneath the armor of outrage. The next time he met with Carlos, he would be sure to have a word with him about honor and decency. And treating women with respect.

Whatever Carlos had done, he'd clearly hurt Cassandra Wells in a way she was still struggling with. Had he cheated on her? Courted her then left her high and dry? It wouldn't be the first time Carlos had behaved badly. Was he now trying to compensate with whatever was in the envelope Julian had just carried across the ocean on his behalf?

There really was no tactful way to ask. She would tell him to mind his own business if he tried. And she'd be right. None of this was any of his concern whatsoever. Other than guilt by association, which seemed to come with the territory when Carlos was involved. Then why did he want so badly to somehow comfort and soothe a woman he'd met barely half an hour ago? A woman who even now held the door open for him so he would leave, tapping her foot impatiently for emphasis.

What choice did he have?

It wasn't as if he could demand to remain in her apartment and insist she disclose all the details. If Carlos was standing in front of him right now, Julian would haul him out into the hallway and give him a good beating. No doubt Carlos deserved it.

Silently, he rose up off the couch. Cassandra wasn't making eye contact. As if she couldn't bear to look at him. He knew it had nothing to do with him personally. Still, it stung. Which was beyond ridiculous if you thought about it.

Making his way to the doorway, he had half a mind to just drop Carlos's envelope "accidentally." But he wasn't going to push, because she said she didn't want it. He would respect that. For now.

But he had to look into all this. Like it or not, he'd been dragged into a situation he couldn't walk away from and still live with himself.

When he got to his car minutes later, Julian yanked his phone out and dialed Carlos's number. The call went straight to voice mail. With a Spanish curse, he disconnected and fired off a text.

Call me as soon as you can. We need to talk.

A response appeared on the screen almost immediately.

Can't talk right now. Were you able to deliver the documents?

Julian responded.

No. And before you ask why, I have my own questions.

Carlos's dialogue bubble floated on the screen for quite a while before his text appeared.

Please try again. Here's a work address for her if you didn't find her at home.

The words were followed by yet another address in Boston.

Julian threw his phone into the passenger seat in frustration. This was useless. He clearly wasn't going to get any kind of answers from his cousin via text. He knew he should just forget the whole thing. He had every right to tell Carlos to figure out another way to achieve whatever it was he was after here.

But Cassandra's fiery defiance and quiet strength had moved him in a way he couldn't really explain. He recalled the shadow of pain in her dark eyes and the grim set of her mouth when she'd realized why Julian was there, and a strange sensation tightened his gut. She wasn't Carlos's usual type. She seemed much more subdued and serious than the flashy, heavily perfumed women Carlos usually had draped over his arm. She certainly didn't appear the type to indulge in meaningless trysts. Which begged the question, did she have deep feelings for his cousin? The tension in his middle grew tighter though he couldn't explain why. What exactly was their story?

One thought hammered in his brain—at least on the surface, Cassandra Wells seemed much too good for the likes of Carlos Alhambra.

Though it made no sense, he'd already decided that he'd check on her once more before he left town. Maybe by then he'd have some answers and be able to explain himself better when he approached her.

Julian just wanted to make sure she was okay. The woman had almost set fire to her apartment, for heaven's sake. He shuddered to think what might have happened if he hadn't gotten there when he had.

Julian rubbed his forehead and started the car. He had to admit he definitely had a pattern. Damn his protective instincts, which seemed to kick in at the most inopportune times. They had not served him well two years ago. Looked like he would never learn.

Still, he knew he wasn't able to turn his back on Cassandra Wells. Not yet anyway.

CHAPTER TWO

"YOU'RE LATE AGAIN, CASSIE."

Cassie halted in her tracks and slowly turned around to face her boss. She'd been hoping to walk by him unnoticed. Though why she'd expected anything to go her way today was a mystery. In fact, things hadn't been going her way for the better part of a month now. She would never regret this baby; it was just tough given the timing and the circumstances.

It had taken her forever to clean the mess in the kitchen. She'd been shaking from shock and fury. The nerve of that man for showing up at her apartment unannounced. And to deliver something from his cousin. He was probably just as bad as Carlos was. Genetics and traits that ran in the family, and all that.

So what if he'd helped her put out what could have been a dangerous kitchen fire? That didn't soothe her fury. And the way he'd been so condescending! Calling her clumsy. Asking why she hadn't thought to offer him water. Her blood pounded in her veins just thinking about it.

Now she had to deal with an irate boss. "Hi, Martin. I'm really sorry. You wouldn't believe what happened earlier this afternoon. It took me forever to clean it up..." She let the sentence trail off when she noted the look on his face. Her boss was not in the mood to listen to any excuses. Fire or no fire.

"Can I see you in my office?" he asked and turned to the small room in the back of the nightclub slash bar where Cassie had worked as operations manager for the better part of two years. Her dream job, in fact. A job she loved and desperately needed now that she would be supporting herself plus one.

She silently followed Martin through the door. He motioned for her to shut it behind her.

"Have a seat," he instructed, though he remained standing.

A proverbial brick settled in Cassie's stomach as she sat down. Martin looked so serious. And determined. She uttered a small prayer under her breath to somehow will away what she was almost certain was about to happen.

She was right. Martin's next words were straight to the point, "I'm afraid I have to let you go."

Oh, no. This couldn't be happening. "Martin, if I could just explain. See, there was a fi—"

He waved away her attempt at an explanation. "I'm surprised you even want to continue here, Cassie. I mean, given your condition."

Her mouth went dry. She'd thought she'd been so discreet. "My condition?"

He nodded, expressionless. "It's pretty obvious. You haven't been yourself. Not for a while now."

"I haven't?"

"No. You've been running to the bathroom every time you have to deliver a meal."

To be fair, she only reacted that way to the daily beef specials. Clearly, this child she was carrying had some kind of an aversion to red meat.

Martin went on. "You're constantly holding your midsection. And you've been uncharacteristically undependable."

Cassie's earlier panic turned to scathing ire. Martin had been clearly watching her closely. And now he was ready to pounce.

"I'm pretty sure there are laws against firing someone for pregnancy, Martin."

He merely shrugged. "Yes. But there are no laws against firings for incompetence."

Incompetence! Cassie had been busting her behind for this club since she'd been hired. And this was the thanks she was going to get?

"I'm sure you don't want to be the pregnant woman walking around the bar, around all those drinks, being shoved around on the dance floor."

Translation: Martin was the one who didn't want a clumsy pregnant woman marring the sea of beautiful people who frequented the Liberty Palace. Everyone, from Boston's sports figures to high-powered attorneys to politicians, was known to spend their weekend evenings here. Martin was concerned about the image his precious club projected.

She decided to play her only hand. "I think you'll be hearing from my attorney," she bluffed, hoping he wouldn't call her on it.

He did. In the worst possible way. "You can

do that, of course. But any kind of suit will have to lay open all sorts of facts about your employment history here."

His words came as a surprise. "But my history's been exemplary." Well, before the past few weeks it had anyway. She just had been hit with the worst morning sickness and had been late a few more times than she would have liked. Still, she'd managed to arrive at work before any real kind of crowd appeared. It was a nightclub, for heaven's sake.

"Has it?"

"Um, yes," Cassie responded, her voice much shakier than she would have liked.

"Really? What about the night that the bachelor party came in?"

Cassie sucked in a breath. The nerve of him to use that night against her. "What transpired during that bachelor party was not my fault. You can't blame me."

Another shrug. "The fact is, you were the one in charge when it all went down." He finally sat down and gave her a level, piercing look. "So I can either give you a recommendation to help you find another position. Or we can have all this come out during some kind of civil proceeding."

Gritting her teeth, she stood so forcefully, her chair nearly toppled backward. "Please email me the recommendation as soon as you can."

Then she left the office without another word. What else was there to say? On top of everything else, now she had a job search on her hands.

Yet one more thing she had to thank Carlos Alhambra for. He was one of the bachelors at that party—the one that had so far turned her whole life upside down.

In more ways than one.

Carlos and his condescending cousin could both go to hell as far as she was concerned.

She was crying.

Julian had no doubt about it. Even from this distance, and the relative darkness of the early fall evening, there was no question Cassie was upset as she left the revolving doors of the establishment she'd entered only moments ago. Some type of dance hall or nightclub. Carlos's text had mentioned she worked at night.

She spotted him just as he approached the entrance. Pure fury shone in her eyes. It was a wonder he wasn't a pile of charred remains on the sidewalk given the heat of her gaze.

"You!"

"Please, just give me a minute." He'd simply wanted to check on her once more to make sure she was okay. Clearly, she wasn't.

"I have to get to the station. I'd like to catch the next train," she threw over her shoulder.

With that, she blew right past him, as if he were a repulsive demon straight out of a horror movie.

"Can we start over?" he asked. "Our initial meeting was a little jarring. What with the flames and all. Even you have to admit that."

She turned on her heel to glare at him. "That's because I'm such a klutz. You said so yourself."

He gave her a slight bow. "I apologize. I have no excuse." Not like he'd walked into an emergency that had completely thrown him off or anything. "I was caught a bit off guard and reacted poorly."

Some of the tightness seemed to leave her face. The lines around her eyebrows softened slightly. He had to acknowledge just how attractive he found her. Soft dark curls framed a heart-shaped face with chocolate brown eyes and elegant eyebrows. Funny, Julian couldn't recall ever noticing a woman's eyebrows before. An aura of determination and strength emanated from her, yet he could also sense a hint of vulnerability.

"Fine. I accept your apology."

He didn't know why that gave him such a sense of relief, as if a tightening in his chest had loosened. "Thank you."

"But I still don't want anything you may have to give me from...you know."

He nodded. "I see. You aren't the least bit curious?"

"I told you I'm not."

"I understand."

She glanced at her watch and swore. Impressively, he would add. "What's the matter?"

"There's no way I'm going to make my train." He watched as her face went pale. "And I just want to get home. But for some reason you keep showing up." She said more but the rest of her words were an incoherent mess. He was fluent but his English skills could only do so much.

To his horror, her tears were flowing steadily now.

"I will get you home, Cassandra. My car is right across the street."

She sniffled and looked him up and down. "No, I don't even know you. Not really. And what I do know of you doesn't exactly make me a fan. I can walk back to my apartment."

He slammed a palm to his chest in mock hurt. "I see I've been found guilty by association. Hardly fair, don't you think?"

"Maybe. But still. Before this afternoon, I'd never so much as laid eyes on you. You don't even know to call me Cassie. Everyone uses that name for me."

He gave her what he hoped was a reassuring smile. "Only one way to fix that, I would think, Cassie."

"What do you mean?"

"Let me buy you a cup of coffee."

Instead of answering, she started to fumble

around in her large purse, clearly looking for something. "I just need a tissue."

Julian waited patiently as she searched unsuccessfully. The woman was in no condition to walk anywhere in her state. One by one, she started handing him various items from her bag as she continued her hunt for the elusive tissue. So far, he held a pocket mirror, a tube of lipstick and a calendar diary. When she absentmindedly handed him a distinctly feminine item, Julian couldn't stand it any longer. Shifting the whole load under his arm, he undid his silk tie and handed it to her.

"Here. Just use this."

She blinked at it. "It looks expensive."

"Please. I insist."

She hesitated still, but not for long. "Thank you. I'll be sure to get it back to you somehow."

"Keep it. It's not even one of my favorites."

She sniffled again. "Thanks again."

"Now, about that cup of coffee? I'd say you could use it." He'd almost asked her if she wanted to get a drink with him, but something told him he shouldn't make that offer.

She blotted her cheeks with his tie then

stared at it as if it held some unknown answer to a deep, burning question.

Finally, she looked up at him. The sheen of tears in her eyes and the look of utter defeat in their depths nearly had him reaching for her. "You know what? Why not?" She laughed out loud then, but it held zero mirth. "What else have I got to do?"

"Ouch. That wasn't the most enthusiastic response I've ever gotten at the prospect of spending time with me."

"I'm afraid it's the best I can do given the circumstances," she said on a deep sigh as she opened her bag and he replaced all her items back in it.

He nodded. "Though it wounds my pride, I'll take it."

Was he imagining things or had he just detected a hint of a smile along her ruby-red lips? She looked away toward the street before he could know for sure. "I have one condition however."

"What's that?"

"Please do not even mention that man's name."

It surprised Julian that it took him a half a

second to realize exactly whom she was referring to.

Their short conversation just now had narrowed his focus to her and her only. Somehow, standing here in the middle of a busy Boston street, as club-goers bustled around them in the latest stylish outfits after they emerged out of late-model sports cars, he'd almost forgotten the exact reason he was here. The underlying reality had simply fled his mind completely when he'd found her crying and upset.

His only focus and his only concern had been for Cassie.

Why was he being so nice to her?

And why did Cassie find it rather unsettling that he was? She had no idea. Her emotions were running roughshod over her ability to think straight. No doubt hormones played a huge role. One minute she was angry and ready to throw something at the man's head. The next, she was accepting his offer to buy her a beverage.

She was about to suggest they head to the

chain coffee shop around the corner when her stomach made a loud, grumbling sound.

Great. First she was a sniveling, red-cheeked mess and now her body was making indiscriminate sounds. How embarrassing. He had to be wondering what any man could have ever seen in her. Let alone someone he was related to.

"I didn't get a chance to eat earlier," she said by way of explanation.

He stopped in his tracks, gently touched her arm. "It just so happens I haven't had a chance to have dinner either. Or lunch, for that matter." He glanced at his watch. "How about I buy you an early dinner instead?"

She really was hungry. Famished, in fact. And after the day she had, a nice hot meal would go a long way toward soothing some of her frazzled nerves. And she'd already agreed to sit down with him. There really was no reason to turn down the offer of dinner. In for a penny and all that.

"Sure, why not?"

The smile he gave her made her heart skip

a beat. "Again with the enthusiasm. You really must try to tamp it down somewhat."

He really was quite a striking specimen of a man. Not that she was noticing men much these days. But Julian had an air of strength about him, a hardness. So that when he smiled, the transformation was a bit remarkable.

Or maybe she was just being fanciful and silly. She had to be careful. The last time she'd fallen for the charms of a handsome, foreign man, her whole world had turned upside down.

He broke into her thoughts. "You appear to be overthinking things, senorita. This will be nothing more than two new acquaintances sharing a meal."

Surprising, how well he'd just read her.

He surprised her further with his next words. "I can assure you, I am nothing like Carlos." She believed him. She didn't see Julian turning a blind eye to any kind of responsibility. Let alone a child he had fathered.

Plus, he was right. She did have a tendency to overanalyze things. Especially now when there was so much more than just herself to consider.

She simply nodded as they resumed walking. "Where would you like to go?" he asked her.

"Depends on what you're in the mood for."

As hungry as she was, she was up for anything. Well, maybe not a rare steak.

Julian continued, "I always enjoy the Changing Scene when I'm in town. And I believe it's within walking distance."

She wasn't surprised that he had just named one of the most exclusive and sought-after Boston restaurants. Not to mention pricey. Even with her satin black wrap dress and sensible leather pumps she might still be considered underdressed for the place.

"I hope you thought to make reservations ahead of time," she told him. "That place is booked out months in advance. Especially this time of year."

He gave her a look of indulgence. "I did not. But we should be able to work something out with the maître d'."

Right. She knew Julian's type well enough. She dealt with his sort all the time in her line of work. He was the kind of man the staff at fancy metropolitan restaurants worked to accommodate. They wouldn't even care if the woman he walked in with wasn't dressed quite appropriately.

She studied him now. Unlike her, he would fit in perfectly at the Changing Scene. Fancy restaurants didn't turn away men like Julian regardless of reservation status. Without the tie, he'd undone his top two buttons. A small V of tanned, olive skin was now revealed beneath a strong chin and neck. The man exuded class and charm. And whatever cologne or aftershave he was wearing practically sent out tangible pheromone waves. Some type of citrus and mint mixture that was making her swoony. Cassie nearly halted in her tracks. She had no business thinking along those lines. Not about him or anyone else, for that matter. She was in no condition to feel any kind of attraction, hormones or not.

Julian seemed to have made the decision about the restaurant and they turned at the next corner. Cassie figured she was about to share a very interesting meal.

A few minutes later, they approached the

doorway of the high-rise building that housed the restaurant. Its name referred to the circular revolving floor at the very top. Along with world-renowned celebrity chefs and spectacular food, it boasted one of the best views of the entire Boston skyline as the entire top floor turned almost imperceptibly in a full circle. She'd only been there once for a work event. And that was just to visit. She'd never actually been able to eat there.

As he'd predicted, they had no trouble being seated, despite the lack of a reservation. In no time, two different servers in tuxedos appeared at the table to take their drink and appetizer orders. Cassie asked for lemon water while Julian ordered a bourbon that probably cost more than her monthly rent.

Looking around her now, she couldn't help but think how naive she'd been to think she and Carlos could have any kind of future together. This was the type of lifestyle he came from. Just like the man who sat across from her now. How could she have thought for even a moment that she would ever be anything more than a fling for someone like him?

"Care to talk about it?" Julian asked, raising his crystal glass and taking a slow sip of the rich amber liquid it contained.

He could be referring to so many things.

"You were obviously very distraught when I caught up to you earlier," he added. "Are you all right?"

She didn't answer but rather posed a question of her own. "How did you find me anyway?"

"I was told to try your place of work if I had no luck at your home."

She should have known. Why did Carlos want him to find her so badly? But she knew the answer to that. As far as Carlos was concerned, she was nothing more than a check mark on his to-do list. He wanted to pay her off then forget about her. Well, she didn't want his money. She refused to accept anything from the man who would so callously turn his back on her in the state she was in. And their unborn child.

She answered Julian on a deep sigh. "That would be my former place of work. It so happens, I was canned when you came by."

"Canned?"

"Fired. Let go. Tossed out on my derriere."

Julian set his glass down. "I see. That explains the tears."

"I needed that job. I loved that job." She felt the sting of tears behind her eyes once more and willed them away. But it was hard to contain the despair. She'd worked so hard through hospitality school and then later as a server. When she'd finally been promoted to the managerial position at one of the hottest nightclubs in the city, it had been no less than a dream come true. All to have it just yanked away because of some ill-timed, impulsive decisions she'd made over a month ago.

With consequences she would be living with for the rest of her life.

Julian studied Cassie across the table and wondered what this pull was that he seemed to be feeling toward her. For one, she certainly did seem to lead an interesting life. Since he'd met her only earlier today, she'd already caused a near disaster in her kitchen then gotten fired a few hours later.

Oh, and there was also that whole thing about her being a former fling of his partying, freewheeling adopted cousin.

What exactly was between them now? Carlos and Cassie? A twinge of something he couldn't name registered in his gut at the thought that there might be something still. But Julian knew enough about his cousin to guess that he'd somehow wronged this woman, then turned his back on her. The thought sent a burst of fury through his core. Cassie didn't deserve to be treated that way by any man. Let alone someone like Carlos.

"I happen to be a very good listener," he said as the waiter arrived with fresh, hot bread. A curl of steam drifted from the basket that was set on the table.

Cassie wasted no time reaching for a slice. The expression of utter pleasure on her face as she took a bite nearly had him chuckling. Either she was really hungry, or she had a clear appreciation for fresh bread. Maybe both.

She shrugged after the first bite. "You mean about why I was fired? Maybe you could ask your cousin."

Ah. He'd suspected as much. Carlos had done something to endanger the woman's livelihood. No doubt he'd sent Julian here to try and make it up to her with some sort of payoff. That sounded like Carlos. But why insist that Julian deliver it personally? Must have been because he'd expected Cassie to be stubborn enough to turn it down. Carlos thought Julian had the type of negotiation skills to make a woman like Cassie budge. Julian would like to think so. But from what he'd seen of her so far, she didn't seem easily swayed. Expert negotiations or not.

"I thought you didn't want to talk about him," he reminded her, wondering if he should go ahead and reveal the full truth to her. That Carlos was not a blood relative. There didn't really seem to be a good way to bring up the matter, however. And what did it really matter in the overall scheme of things?

She took another bite of the bread. "I don't. You asked me about getting fired. He played a huge role in that turn of events."

"Maybe you could tell me about it in general terms," he prompted.

She set her slice down and looked him in the eye. "All right. Let's say that when a group of unruly partiers shows up at your club for a bachelor party that no one thought to book ahead of time, and then gets rowdy, loud and destructive, it's looked upon as an abject failure of the manager on duty that night."

"I see. I take it you were that night manager."

She gave a mocking, slow clap. "Give the man a prize."

"Were the damages that costly?" he asked her.

"They were enough."

Another reason Carlos was trying to compensate her. The costs of repairs must have come out of Cassie's pay. For once in his life, Carlos was trying to do something right. Julian had to admit to being surprised. It wasn't something that happened often.

"That hardly seems like a rare occurrence at a nightclub," he told her. "I would think your supervisor might have given you some leeway."

"He might have. If the unauthorized strippers hadn't shown up later. That's a severe permitting offense."

"I'm really sorry, Cassie. I hope they had the decency to at least apologize."

Something darkened behind her eyes.

"Oh, Carlos apologized all right." Her mouth formed a thin line.

There was so much more to the story, he could tell. Julian hoped she'd feel inclined to share the rest with him at some point. He wanted her to trust him, though he couldn't explain quite why. He'd only just met the woman. But he wasn't going to push her. Not yet. It seemed Cassie had been pushed enough already for one day.

With a fortunate bout of timing, the server appeared to take their dinner order. He opted for the aged rib eye while Cassie chose the Chilean sea bass.

She continued, staring off at the horizon outside the glass wall of the restaurant, "When I think about how hard I worked for that place... I can't believe they just tossed me aside." Her lips quivered slightly. "Just last week I caught an error with the wine order before it was put through. We would have faced a disastrous shortage if it had gone unnoticed." She sniffled. "I did everything for that man. I monitored spirits inventory, booked entertainment, handled clientele when they got unruly. Not to mention going in early and staying until the break of dawn to clean up after closing. And this is the thanks I get."

He wanted to reach out to her, to try and soothe her somehow. Whomever she'd been reporting to seemed to be extremely short-sighted to let an employee like her go.

"Enough about me," she suddenly declared and grabbed another piece of bread. "I'd rather talk about something else."

"What would you like to talk about?"

"You. Tell me about yourself. What brings you to Boston? I take it you live in Spain too."

"Correct. I'm here to meet with one of my suppliers. He prefers face-to-face interaction. A bit of a traditionalist when it comes to business."

"Suppliers?"

"Yes, of high-end fixtures for luxury resorts and hotels. I've been using him for years now. The relationship has worked out well."

"You're in the hospitality business too," she confirmed, taking a sip of her lemon water.

"That's right. I'm opening a new resort. On a small Mediterranean island off the coast of Spain. A one-of-a-kind island paradise."

"Sounds luxurious." A faraway expression

settled over her face. "I've always wanted to visit the Mediterranean coast."

"You should plan on a visit once it's up and running, then. Perhaps once you've secured your professional situation."

She threw her head back and scoffed. "Ha! As if I could ever afford that. I'm not one of those people who'll ever be a guest at a fancy island resort. Especially now..." Her sentence trailed off.

An idea popped into his head that on the surface should have made no sense. But Julian had come a long way in business relying on his instincts. So far, they'd served him well. And he was desperately understaffed at the resort he was trying to have open by the start of next season. He could use all the help he could get.

Her dismissal notwithstanding, Cassie had been in charge of running and managing a major metropolitan nightclub that attracted the likes of millionaires like Carlos and his friends. High-end clientele exactly like the kind he hoped to attract. And he happened to need a woman for this particular position.

He didn't give himself any more time to

think. Some of the best moves of his professional life were born of snap decisions made on the spot. "Well, if you can't see yourself as a guest at such a place, what about as an employee?"

She gave a quick shake of her head. "I don't follow."

Fully trusting his gut, Julian threw down his offer. "Come work for me."

CHAPTER THREE

CASSIE FIGURED SHE couldn't have heard him correctly. "I'm sorry. But I think I misunderstood. It almost sounded like you just offered me a job." Now that she'd said the words out loud, she couldn't help but laugh. There was no way that could be right. Could pregnancy hormones affect one's hearing ability?

"You heard perfectly. I did just offer you a position. Come and work for me. I'm desperately understaffed while I try to get this new resort up and running."

Cassie could only stare at him with her mouth open as their salads were delivered. What could possibly be his play here? He didn't know her from Eve.

"You mean the new resort off the coast of Spain? How am I supposed to do that? I live here, in Boston. I can't just pack up and leave."

"Why not?"

Wasn't it obvious? She had a life here. Didn't she? She paused to analyze that comment, to weigh exactly how true it was. She was currently unemployed, she had no family to speak of—heaven only knew where her mother called home these days. Zara was her only friend but she traveled constantly for work.

How many times had she dreamed of just this kind of opportunity?

"We could make it a temporary position," Julian continued. "Until the resort is fully up and running."

"Temporary?"

He nodded. "Maybe a month or so."

Cassie opened her mouth to speak, to flatly tell him no, once and for all. His offer made no sense whatsoever. How in the world was she supposed to work for Carlos's cousin? What if they were alike at all? She shook off that thought as soon as it arose. Studying Julian across her now, the two men appeared to be polar opposites despite the many physical similarities. Whereas Carlos practically oozed charisma and charm, there was a boyishness underneath. There was absolutely nothing boyish about Julian. In contrast, he exuded a hardness, an edginess she'd be hard-pressed to describe. Carlos was attractive in the classic sense—tall, dark and handsome. Julian's allure included all that and something else that was much subtler.

Stop it. She had to stop comparing the two of them.

The wisest thing to do in response to Julian's offer was to flat out reject it. But what were her other options? It could take weeks to find another job. In the meantime, she'd have to pay for health care, now that she was unemployed. As far as her pregnancy was concerned, her next medical appointment wasn't for another month. Exactly the duration Julian had just suggested.

She could certainly use the money. And she could always search for and apply to local jobs online while she actually earned some income.

Still. This was happening much too fast. She'd only just met the man this morning for heaven's sake.

"Why me? You just met me."

"I don't really have the time to conduct any

kind of professional search. I've got a hiring services department but they're taking much too long. I'd like to get at least this one position filled as soon as possible."

"That doesn't really answer my question. Why me?"

He gave a small shrug as he took another sip of his drink. "Everything you've told me so far about your professional background makes you a perfect fit for the position. In fact, I'm wondering how I got so lucky."

Lucky. Well, that made one of them. Cassie stabbed a plum tomato with her fork, contemplating his words. Was she crazy to even consider his offer? A month spent on a Spanish island in the Mediterranean sounded like heaven. She could certainly use a getaway. Under any other circumstances, she would jump at the opportunity. But there was so much more to consider now than just herself.

Still, she couldn't bring herself to say no. Not yet anyway. "You have to understand, I'll need some time to think about all this. And it's highly unlikely that I'll agree in the end."

The smile he gave her made something catch at the base of her throat. *Oh, no. Don't*

even think about it. She absolutely could not
go there. No matter how charming Julian's
smile was. God, wasn't her life complicated
enough as it was? If she did entertain his
proposition, it was nothing more than business. And it was a big *if.*

"But you're not saying no," he said and
raised his glass, as if in a mini salute.

"I guess I'm not. Not yet anyway."

He reached for his phone. "Excellent. I'll
have my office email over the documents
right away." Cassie heard the sound of a text
being sent.

He seemed to move quickly. Working for a
man like that could be harrowing and overly
demanding under the best of circumstances.
Cassie wondered if she could even hope to
keep up.

Julian felt an almost ridiculous sense of opti-
mism that she may take him up on his offer.
Now that he'd made it, he felt more and more
convinced that it was a shrewd business decision. Not only would it save him time, he
knew with Cassie he'd be hiring a hardwork-

ing, dedicated professional who knew what she was doing.

He wouldn't divulge to her that he'd done a quick search on her after leaving her apartment, his curiosity beyond piqued. She didn't have much of an online presence, not on social media anyway. But a couple of professional networking websites had complimentary profiles about her. Additionally, a city magazine had done a write-up last year about up-and-coming young professionals and she was one of the locals profiled. She had no way to know it, but he would have never made such a proposition without knowing her professional history.

Though he couldn't count his winnings just yet. She hadn't actually agreed. He would just have to try and sell a little harder while he had the chance. He was offering her a job in paradise and would pay her handsomely.

Cassie still seemed deep in thought by the time they'd finished their meals. He'd given her a lot to think about. She spoke again after several silent minutes. "Why would I accept a job offer from someone I just met?" she wanted to know. "All I know about you is that you're *his* cousin."

He'd have had to be deaf to miss the disdain in her tone as she'd uttered the one word.

"Well, not exactly."

She squinted at him. "I don't follow."

Julian set his fork down. Carlos's place in the Santigo family was rather unconventional. Even after all these years, it took some explaining whenever someone asked.

"We are not actually blood relatives. I refer to him as a cousin as do my two younger brothers. My mother calls him her nephew."

Cassie blinked up at him, clearly seeking more answers. For a subject she asked not to discuss, Carlos was about to take up a lot of the conversation.

"We grew up together in the same household after Carlos lost both his parents in a small-plane accident. His mother was a close friend of my own *madre*."

Understanding seemed to dawn in her eyes. "Your family took him in."

Julian nodded. "Correct. He was barely thirteen. I'd just turned sixteen. We all viewed him as part of the family. But Carlos was uncomfortable with being referred to that way. He said he lost his own real family in the plane accident. Insisted that he wasn't our brother or son. So he became a 'cousin,' so to speak."

"I see. So Carlos was sort of adopted and lived with your parents and brothers."

He nodded. "For a while."

"Only a while?" Cassie asked.

Julian worked hard to keep the inflection of emotion out of his voice when he answered. Even after all these years, it wasn't easy to do so. "Then I lost my own father."

Cassie's gasp was as soft as a whisper. "I'm sorry, Julian." The wealth of sympathy in her voice felt like a soothing caress.

"*Gracias.* It was rather unexpected. Undiagnosed heart condition. So it was just me, my brothers and Carlos living with my mother."

Cassie's eyes softened. For one insane moment he thought she may reach for his hand across the table. A part of him wished she would do just that. "Let me guess, you're the oldest?"

She was astute, no doubt about it. "Yes. How did you know?"

Cassie merely shrugged. "It's easy enough to guess. The way you carry yourself. I get the feeling you took over a lot of the responsibility in your father's absence." She quickly cupped her palm to her mouth, as if realizing she may have said too much. "I'm sorry, I shouldn't have…"

He held a hand up to stop her apology. "It's okay. You're correct in your assumption. As the oldest, I felt like I had to do more to make up for my father's loss. To my mother as well as my brothers and Carlos."

Not for the first time, he had to wonder if he hadn't failed as far as the latter was concerned. Carlos wasn't exactly a paragon of integrity. Julian couldn't help feeling partly responsible for the man his cousin had turned out to be. Perhaps he could have done more to help shape his character. Julian had bailed him out of more than one tricky situation. Maybe he should have left Carlos to his own devices during some of those instances. Maybe he might have learned a lesson or two.

He looked up to find Cassie studying him.

Their conversation had taken a turn Julian wouldn't have expected. They'd just met, but somehow they were both in tune with each other enough to feel a sense of familiarity. She was certainly easy to talk to.

Slowly and gradually, the city lights below them started to come on as the evening grew later. By the time they were handed their dessert menus, Boston's skyline resembled a scene out of a painting. Both of them declined, though Julian was tempted to order something simply to prolong the dinner.

It dawned on him as he paid the bill that he didn't want the evening to end. Usually, he'd be champing at the bit to get back to his hotel room and get caught up on all the emails and tasks that always seemed never-ending. Instead, he found he just wanted a few more hours to put all that responsibility off, just for a while longer. In the company of the woman sitting across him.

He'd just shared more about himself with Cassie Wells than he had with anyone else in all his adulthood.

The lights in the dining room had grown dimmer throughout their meal as their evening grew later. The candle at the center of the table cast shadows on Cassie's face and accentuated her jet-black hair and dark brown eyes. She really was a very beautiful young lady. Her looks were striking in a way that turned heads. But she seemed completely unaware of the fact.

She had so much going for her. With a bright future ahead.

Too bad the same couldn't be said about him.

"I'll get you back to your apartment," he told her, after failing to come up with a way to prolong the evening.

Her next words had him wondering if perhaps she was thinking along the same lines.

"Do you mind if we take the long way back walking to your car?" She ducked her head as soon as she asked the question, as if she'd debated whether or not to do so. "I could use some air," she added in a lower voice.

"Of course." Julian rose and walked to her side, pulling out her chair as she got up. "I think that's a great idea, especially after the heavy meal I just had."

"Thanks. I'm not really looking forward to going back to my place, actually."

"Oh? Why's that?" Julian asked as they made their way to the elevator.

She sighed. "I did my best to clean up the mess after the fire, but it still smelled like charred plaster and fabric when I left this afternoon. I suspect it'll linger for a few days. And opening the windows is only going to let more odor in, between the city streets and the bay nearby."

He chuckled. "Sensitive to smells, are you?"

Something shifted behind her eyes right before she looked away. "Something like that," she said in a voice so low he almost couldn't hear her. "I wasn't always," she added, then muttered something else under her breath even more softly. She was talking to herself.

"Beg your pardon?" he asked her.

But the elevator doors swished open before she answered and then she stepped inside silently. Within moments, they had reached the ground floor of the building and exited outside into the balmy bayside air. The streets and sidewalks had grown more crowded as they'd dined. The evening was in full gear now. Various strands of music could be heard from more than a few different directions. Car horns blared amidst muddled conversations. A street artist was working on a chalk portrait several feet away. Julian always considered Boston to be a fun city with plenty to do and enjoy throughout the year.

He felt a strange pang of regret in his gut. For just one insane second, he wished this evening was more than what it actually was. That he and Cassie were out on some kind of first date. That they'd just shared a romantic dinner getting to know each other before he was about to take her dancing. He imagined she'd be an ideal dance partner, her movements fluid and graceful. And when a slower song came on, he imagined her stepping into his arms on the dance floor. Allowing him to hold her tight as they gently swayed together.

Dios! Enough already. He wasn't a child playacting. What was wrong with him?

He had no intention of dating or dancing with any woman anytime soon. The wounds and scars of the recent past were still far too fresh. He wouldn't let a woman romantically entice him again. He had far too much to do with this resort opening. And besides all that, he knew better.

So, his next words to Cassie surprised him down to his toes. "You said you weren't exactly thrilled at the prospect of going back to your apartment. Why don't you come back to my hotel?"

Cassie stopped in her tracks with a loud gasp. "Come again?"

Julian paused before her and gave a shake of his head. "I'm sorry. It's the language gap."

"I don't understand."

"I only mean to show you some paperwork and brochures, some more detail about what the job would involve. So that you could have a better idea and make a more informed decision. I could bring it down to the lobby to peruse over a drink perhaps."

She was about to tell him the drink part was out of the question, for one. But it was tough to come up with an appropriate segue. Besides, she was still trying to process that he was close with Carlos but merely called him a cousin. They weren't related by blood. In the overall scheme of things, the fact hardly made a difference. What had struck her as more important was that he'd taken over as patriarch of a rather complicated family once he'd lost his father. She couldn't help but feel a sense of admiration.

He continued, "It might be beneficial to go over it together rather than emailing you a file to look over by yourself."

On the surface, it made sense. Except when one considered that the whole concept was a foregone conclusion. She could not in any possible way accept a position halfway across the world on such short notice.

"I don't think that's a good idea," she told him. A completely true statement. So why was she so tempted by the offer to go back to his hotel with him?

Loneliness. That's all this was. She was simply lonely. Nothing like expecting a baby to make a woman realize exactly how solitary in the world she really was. Not that it was anything new for her. But it hurt to think that her child would be brought into the world under those same circumstances.

The problem now was the little voice at the back of her mind poking at her again. That same voice that told her to stop analyzing every decision and every thought. The last time she had listened to that voice, it had gotten her into her current unexpected state. But this was an entirely different scenario, wasn't it?

This man had just made her a job offer. Nothing more. He simply wanted to discuss it with her. Not that she was seriously considering accepting. The possibility was out of the question. She was only tempted because of a reluctance to go back to her cramped, dingy apartment which now smelled of a combination of old, wet bonfire and various cleaning solvents.

"You'll have to excuse my forwardness," Julian said. "It's just that I'm a bit short on time if I want to stay on schedule with this opening."

That explained why he would make such an offer to a virtual stranger. So, she shouldn't even consider flattering herself.

"I'm not usually so…what's the word?" he asked after a pause.

"Pushy?"

His bark of laughter tickled her and she couldn't suppress a small giggle.

"Not the word I would have chosen, but I suppose it works."

The man was downright breathtaking when he laughed. His dark eyes sparkled and lit his face. His angular jawline sported the faintest five-o'clock shadow, adding a look of sharp edginess to his already striking face.

More than a few women stared as they walked by. Julian seemed completely unaware of their attention, as if he was used to it all. It occurred to her that to an outside observer they may appear to be a couple out on a date. Or one already intimate with each other.

The truth was so very opposite. Her dating days were effectively over, for the foreseeable future anyway.

"I guess I'll drop you off back at your place, then," he said after an awkward silence. She was probably only imagining the hint of disappointment framing his eyes.

"I think that would be best."

They walked the next half a block in silence. Cassie couldn't help but throw several furtive glances his way. He certainly had the kind of looks that made women stare. And like the ladies they passed on the sidewalk, she was no different.

"Thanks again for dinner," she said, simply to get some words flowing between them again and to try and refocus.

"You're welcome. I should thank you, as well."

That was rather curious. "Why is that?"

He shrugged. "Dining with a lovely woman such as yourself certainly beats sitting on a hotel couch scarfing down room service while answering a thousand emails."

Wow. What a charmer. If she wasn't careful, she would find herself basking in his compliments.

Probably a cultural thing. Julian probably wasn't even aware of how charming he was. Again, no need to flatter herself. Still, it was rather intriguing to think that loneliness might be a factor for him, as well. Not that it was even remotely the same. He was traveling on business alone in a city far from home. He came from a large family who evidently depended on him. He ran an international business with a myriad of employees who also depended on him.

By contrast, Cassie was by herself and lonely in the city she called home.

The same persistent voice popped up again in the back of her mind. This time she only managed to swat it away briefly before it resurfaced. Louder than before. Far too loud to ignore much longer.

She paused once again. Julian stopped as well and turned to her. "Something wrong?"

Yes! she wanted to scream. Everything was totally wrong. She was pregnant and scared and by herself. As much as she wanted and already loved this baby, the radical life change she was facing had her shaking internally with fear and anxiety. With no one to turn to for comfort or to confide in.

The familiar serpent of doubt and self-reproach reared its ugly head once more.

What if she couldn't do it? What if she failed at the most important role she'd ever had to take on in her life so far?

She knew it was foolish to follow Julian

back to his hotel as he'd asked, but at the least, it would give her a short reprieve from the catastrophic thoughts jumbled in her brain. He'd proven an effective distraction from the moment he'd walked into her apartment earlier today. Was it so wrong to want that distraction just a bit longer?

She'd learned a bit about him over dinner. He seemed less of a stranger now. She'd learned he was someone who came through when others needed him. So different from what she'd experienced from the man he called his cousin.

Now he stood staring at her. Right, he'd asked her a question. Sucking in a deep breath, Cassie counted silently to ten. Every once in a while she would experience these sudden surges in apprehension. Episodes in which her constant low-level anxiety turned to all-out panic. She'd come perilously close to one just now.

"I've reconsidered," she announced, willing her voice to sound steady and composed. Despite her better judgment, she'd decided to take him up on the offer to go back to his hotel. She wasn't going to go any farther than the lobby. What could be the harm in that? "I think I would rather like to come discuss the job some more with you."

CHAPTER FOUR

JULIAN HAD NO idea where the change of heart came from. Just that he was absurdly glad for it. Not that he could explain why. All she'd agreed to really was hearing him out about the job. But he was confident enough in his negotiation skills that the small window of a chance increased his prospects dramatically. He would pull every tool in his skills bag to try and persuade her. Something about this woman called to him, triggered all his protective instincts in a way he didn't want to examine. There was a story there. Most likely one that involved his cousin. But he wasn't going to go in search of it. This was about filling an opening in his business. Nothing more. Every cell in his body told him she was perfect for the role.

He studied Cassie now. Her cheeks were flushed, her breathing quickened. Any other time, in any other place, he might have pursued something romantic with the woman he stood across. There was no doubt she was alluring, sexy in a way she didn't even seem to realize. Her dark coloring and rather curvy figure screamed enticement.

He pushed the thought away before it could go any further. Instead, he held out his arm. "Let's waste no time, then, senorita. I'm going to get you to the hotel before you change your mind."

She flashed him a dazzling smile before taking his arm. Within moments, they had reached the rented silver Mercedes.

It took another twenty minutes of struggling through congested Boston traffic before he finally reached the valet service in front of the Harbor Hotel. He guided Cassie inside as he tossed the uniformed attendant the car key fob.

A server approached as soon as they were seated in a wide-open lounge area on the first floor.

"Shall I get us a bottle of wine?" he asked Cassie. "This might take a while."

She declined immediately with a sharp shake of her head. "Just a lemonade for me."

Clearly, she wasn't much of a drinker. She'd only had ice water at the restaurant. "In that case, I'll have one of your local craft beers," he told the young lady before turning back to Cassie.

"I'll run up to my suite to get the brochures and development documents. Be back before our drinks arrive."

"I'll be right here," she answered, resting her head back against the cushy velvet chair.

Julian was more excited than he cared to admit. Presenting the idea behind the Paraiso resort to Cassie would be something of a first. Aside from family, only investors, hired employees and his marketing firm were aware of the concept behind the luxury island getaway. Cassie would be the first American to learn of it, in fact. Funny, he hadn't even thought to insist on a formal nondisclosure agreement before he shared the information with her. That thought gave him pause. Too late to do anything about it now.

The plan really was a novel one. His latest resort would be one of a kind. He couldn't wait to see Cassie's reaction when he told her the specifics. He made quick work of finding the necessary materials when he reached his hotel suite, ensuring to grab the English copies of everything.

He arrived just as their server set a frosty bottle of beer and a tall glass of lemonade on the table in front of Cassie.

"That didn't take long," she said as he sat down next to her.

"I'm a man of my word."

"Pretty rare trait these days," she half muttered.

"I beg your pardon?"

"Never mind." She took a small sip of her drink. "Where do we start?"

"Let's start with a question, shall we?"

"Shoot."

"How many trips have you been on as a single young lady when all you wanted to do was relax without worrying about any kind of unwanted attention?"

Her smile faltered. "I didn't get much of a chance to travel when I was younger. But what do you mean by 'unwanted attention'?"

"Say from interested men."

Her eyes narrowed on him. "What exactly

are you getting at, Julian? What does that have to do with a job on your new resort?"

He reached for one of the brochures. "Here. Let me show you." Opening up to the first page, he waited as she read the print. Her mouth formed a small O before she looked back up at him.

"This says 'Women Guests Only.'"

He nodded at her. "That's right. No men or boys."

"Is that allowed? Is it even legal?"

"It certainly is."

She looked back at the brochure. "All right. Consider me intrigued."

"I had no doubt you would be." Without thinking, he reached for her hand. A jolt of electric current seemed to flare where his palm met her fingers. He quickly pulled back.

Her gaze fell to where he'd touched her before she spoke. "Tell me more."

"The resort is located off the eastern coast of Mallorca. Geared toward female travelers only who are looking for a luxury vacation that combines relaxation, spa treatments, fitness offerings and exposure to local culture. With their girlfriends or their sisters or mothers."

"Strictly women?" she asked again, as if incredulous.

"Correct. No men."

"Huh."

Julian had to believe he had her where he wanted her. Not surprising. Cassie appeared to be a clever and bright young lady who knew a rare opportunity when she stumbled upon it. He just needed to guide her toward making a final commitment.

"You'd be assisting me in the general manager duties. Making sure guests are comfortable and helping to smooth over wrinkles that arise with any new endeavor such as this."

"I see."

"As you might guess, ideally, I would hire a woman in the role. A woman with qualifications just like yours." He flipped a page to show her the room setup. "You'd be provided with accommodations right on the property."

Cassie didn't reply, simply studied the information in front of her.

"And I'm ready to pay handsomely for your talent." Pulling the silver pen out of his jacket pocket, he wrote a figure in US dollars on the cocktail napkin, more than ready to go higher if required.

Her only response was a rather loud gasp.

Cassie stared at the number Julian had just penned in his elegant handwriting on the white napkin. Could he possibly mean this would be the annual salary? But he'd been clear she'd only be a temporary employee for about a month or so. Then it occurred to her what the confusion might be. She wasn't exactly up-to-date on the exchange rate. What was the Euro up to these days anyway?

"You have a dollar sign printed here," she pointed out, waiting for him to correct it.

He didn't move his pen. "That's right."

Okay. Maybe he did mean a yearly salary and expected her to do some quick math in her head. If that was the case, the amount still didn't make any sense.

She rubbed her head. It was getting late after a rather long and arduous day. She wished he would just get to the point. Her curiosity had been piqued and she wanted to hear more. What Julian had described was such a novel and original setup for a resort. Something like that would never fly in the States. A hum of excitement traveled through her veins at the thought of being involved with this kind of project, even temporarily.

Julian tapped his finger on the cocktail napkin. "That would be your compensation for one month of your time. In addition to travel expenses and lodging. If you'd like to counter, I'm listening."

Counter? Was he serious? The amount in question was more than she'd hope to make in half a year's time at her current salary. It was almost too good to be true. This was all happening too fast. Her hormones were wreaking havoc on her ability to think straight. Somehow, she'd walked into a job offer from a man she hadn't even known existed twenty-four hours ago. A man who happened to have a strong connection to the father of the child she carried. The complications were dizzying.

Julian's phone buzzed in his suit pocket. He fished it and glanced at the screen, then stood.

"I need to take this," he told her. "Look everything over once more. I'll be right back."

"Take your time," she managed to utter as he walked away.

Julian disconnected his call and made his way back to the lounge area, eager to resume his negotiation with Cassie, if it was even that at this point. He wasn't one to play games and had offered her a hefty sum from the very get-go. He didn't believe in starting low, considered such maneuvers a waste of time. The sooner they agreed on a sum, the sooner they could move on to the next phase, that being Cassie's ultimate decision.

When he reached her side, it was clear they wouldn't be discussing any kind of agreement any more tonight. Cassie was sound asleep, nearly doubled over sideways in her chair. She didn't look comfortable in the least. He was surprised she could have fallen asleep in that position. Not to mention, given the loud music of a live jazz band in the hotel pub merely feet away.

With a sigh of resignation, he walked back over to the front desk.

"I'd like to reserve an additional room," he told the singular employee behind the counter.

"I'm so sorry, Mr. Santigo. I'm afraid we're all booked for the night."

"Completely?"

The young woman nodded. "Yes. One hundred percent capacity. There's a major concert in town as well as the baseball game."

"I see," Julian answered absentmindedly.

"We're playing New York," she added. "Full stadium."

That certainly explained the traffic nightmare on the way over. He glanced over to where Cassie still hadn't moved from her half lying, half sitting position. She was bound to have more than a few aches and pains and most likely a headache if she remained that way much longer. She must have been exhausted to fall asleep so deeply under these conditions. A glance at his watch told him the hour was much later than he would have guessed.

Time seemed to fly since he'd met Cassie Wells.

He reached her side and gently nudged her

on the shoulder. It took several more tries before she even stirred. She blinked once and again and studied her surroundings as if realizing for the first time exactly where she was. Clearly in the grips of sleep confusion.

"What happened?"

"You fell asleep."

Her response was a wide, long yawn. That settled it. She was in no shape for any kind of drive back to her apartment. Rooms or no rooms. He had ample space in his suite.

"Why don't you stay here? At the hotel."

"Here?" She rubbed her eyes and rested her head back against her seat. "I can't afford a room here." Her words were followed by an even longer yawn.

"I have a suite with two rooms. There's plenty of space for both of us."

Her hesitation was clear in her drowsy, heavy-lidded eyes.

"Both doors lock from the inside with a secure bolt," he reassured her. "And both rooms have comfortable king-size beds."

Her eyebrow lifted ever so slightly. "With plush, cushy pillows?"

"Absolutely." He nodded with a smile then

held his hand out to help her up. She took it without a word and followed him to the main elevator.

Was that really sunshine outside her window already? It couldn't be. She'd just closed her eyes only minutes ago. Cassie grunted and tossed over to her side. Julian had been right about the comfortable luxury bed. She'd almost fought him about staying here last night. But she couldn't remember ever being quite so tired. It seemed silly to insist on leaving at that hour, especially after she'd confirmed his statement about the sturdy door bolt. Plus, if Julian was some kind of crazy maniac who wanted to harm her, he'd had ample opportunity both in her apartment and all the time she'd spent with him in his car. In the end, she was grateful he'd asked her to stay. She really hadn't been looking forward to stepping into her apartment and dealing with the stench of burn. Not to mention, last night might have been the most restful night of sleep she'd gotten since finding out about the baby. And heavens, she'd needed it.

But now, it was time to leave. And she still

had to figure out exactly what to say to Julian about the job. He was probably wondering why she wasn't jumping at the chance. It was a dream of an opportunity. But the circumstances were beyond complicated. Rising with a weary sigh, she made her way to the bathroom to freshen up. She'd slept in her underwear and a silk robe that had been hanging in the closet. A quick shower first, because she couldn't bring herself to resist the luxury dual headed stall, and then she would have to make her way back to reality.

She would have to call a car service. Julian had been inconvenienced enough. When she made her way to the outer suite twenty minutes later, his door was still closed and there was no discernible sound coming from the other side.

Cassie hesitated in the center of the room. She hadn't had a chance to really notice it last night but the suite was about the size of her whole apartment. That's where the similarities ended. The ivory white couch in the center probably cost more than her yearly rent. A wide screen TV as thin as a painting hung on the wall. Plush thick carpet beneath her feet tickled her toes. She felt she might have stepped into a magazine spread.

And she thought the room she'd slept in was luxurious. Julian certainly knew how to live in style.

Should she knock on his door? It seemed rude to just leave without thanking him. Though what if he was still asleep? Before she had a chance to come to any kind of decision, someone else knocked on the main door of the suite, followed by a loud, accented male voice.

"Room service."

Julian's door flung open in the next instant. "Just a min—" He paused when he saw her. "You're awake."

She could only nod. Words failed her. Julian stood with nothing but a thick, white towel wrapped around his waist.

"Do you mind getting that?" he asked, motioning to the main door. "I'm not quite dressed yet."

Still, she couldn't speak. Her mouth had gone dry. The man looked like something out of a cologne ad. His dark olive skin still glistened with moisture from his shower. A chiseled chest sported a smattering of dark hair. He hadn't shaved yet and the shadow of a beard accented his angular jaw. His jet-black wet hair fell in haphazard waves around his face. And his physique. Heavens. How could she not have noticed even under his suit jacket just how muscular he was?

That same, now familiar soap or aftershave he wore had her inhaling deeply to fully take in the rich, masculine scent. Her fingers actually tingled with the desire to reach over and brush the wayward curls off his face then trail along his jaw, perhaps go even farther, lower.

Cassie gave her head a brisk shake. What in the world was wrong with her? It had to be the hormones coursing through her body. There was no way she would otherwise be standing here ogling Julian Santigo of all people. She'd sworn off men, at least for the time being. Her life was in complete disarray right now. The last thing she needed was to lust after a man so completely, utterly off-limits.

"Cassie?" he asked, studying her through narrowed eyes.

She managed to make her mouth work somehow. "Yes?"

"Could you get that?"

It was hard to focus. "Get what?"

He gestured with his chin toward the door. "It's room service. I ordered us some coffee and pastries."

Some of her sense finally kicked in. "Oh! Of course."

She turned on her heel and let the man in, willing her pulse to slow down. The aroma of rich, steamy coffee helped. She still allowed herself one small cup a day. This morning, the caffeine was definitely needed.

By the time the deliverer left, Cassie was finally starting to get a hold of herself.

"Help yourself." Julian stepped out of his room, his hair now combed back. He was dressed in a crisp white shirt with charcoal gray pressed slacks. His sleeves were rolled up to reveal the toned arms she'd been admiring just moments ago. Cassie forced her mind to focus on other things. A steaming, fluffy croissant luckily proved to be an adequate distraction. She indulged in the fresh bread aroma of it before taking a small bite.

The pastry practically melted in her mouth. Despite the large meal last night, she found she was starved. Yet another change. She was the type of person who normally didn't even eat breakfast in the past. Now she couldn't leave for the day without some kind of nourishment.

Julian walked over to pour steamy hot coffee into two porcelain mugs.

"Thank you," she began. "I mean for all of it. It did me a world of good to be able to sleep here last night."

"You did appear quite spent." He handed her one of the mugs. He'd poured generously. She would have to stop at half a cup. Plus, it smelled rather strongly brewed.

So much to think about.

"I didn't mean to doze off on you last night," she began. "It's just that I haven't been sleeping very well lately. I guess it finally caught up to me."

"I'm glad you were able to get some rest, then."

So was she. The events of last night seemed almost unreal. As if she'd just imagined them. At some point during the evening, she'd found herself comfortable and relaxed around Julian. So much so that she'd fallen asleep as she'd waited for him in the hotel lobby. Or perhaps that had been merely due to weeks of exhaustion finally taking its toll.

"Me too. I've been a bit of an insomniac lately. So a good night's sleep was a very welcome reprieve."

A dark eyebrow lifted over his speculative gaze. "Anything in particular keeping you up?"

Cassie almost guffawed out loud at the question. If he only knew.

"I've got a lot on my mind, I guess." That was the complete truth. Cassie found herself wanting to confide in him, something about Julian pulled at her, like a magnetic beam from miles away. Under different circumstances, they might very well have been good friends. Perhaps even more.

That thought had her shaking her head. Useless and wayward thoughts like that one could lead down dangerous paths. No way she could share her predicament with Julian. No matter how badly she could use someone to talk to right now.

"I've got very broad shoulders," he said, the statement so out of the blue, and so in line with her internal thoughts, she couldn't suppress a chuckle.

"I beg your pardon?"

Julian scrunched up his face. "Sorry, that was an attempt at an English idiom. I clearly got it wrong."

Ah, now she understood. It was as if he'd read her mind. "You mean I can confide in you if I want."

He nodded. "Yes! That's what I meant exactly. I have some time before my meeting. If you'd like to talk."

"A shoulder to lean on."

"Precisely." He smiled at her and she couldn't help but feel sheer pleasure move from her chest down to her toes. What curious effect did this man have on her? In such a short period of time, no less.

Maybe she could confide in him, using general terms. He certainly didn't need to know details. Blowing out a breath, she tried to summon the right words. "Let's just say the loss of my job was probably the last thing I needed. And it's so unfair. I worked really hard to get to where I am. Where I was," she corrected. "Now I have to start all over."

"It wasn't easy for you to get there, was it?"

She shook her head, surprised at how easy it was to let it all flow out of her. "No. It wasn't. It took a lot of time and effort." She thwacked her forehead as soon as the words left her mouth. She was perilously close to self-pity territory. Something she refused to accept. "Ugh! Listen to me. I don't mean to sound so sorry for myself."

"You just lost a job you loved. I'd say you have a right to." He crossed his arms in front of his chest. "What about your parents? Were they any help at all to you?"

She shook her head. "I don't really have any parents. I never knew my father." She had to swallow down a hiccup of grief. In a classic case of history repeating itself, her baby would say those exact same words someday.

Before she could process it, Julian had strode over to where she stood and taken her hand in his. His touch felt soothing and comforting. Yet, there was a layer of heat and a spark of electricity that she couldn't ignore.

She resisted the urge to pull away, taking the comfort he offered.

"And your mother?"

"She appeared in and out of my life. Yanking me out from whatever foster home I happened to be assigned to. Swearing she'd changed, that she was ready for the responsibility of a child."

"And that was false?"

Cassie had to laugh. "Yes. Her lucid moments never lasted. Only served to disrupt any semblance of routine I may have started with a substitute family in foster care."

His thumb rubbed the palm of the hand he held. "You truly are a remarkable woman, Cassie. I hope you realize that."

The world seemed to stand still around them as he said the words. Cassie found her mouth had gone dry. Not that she'd have the appropriate response anyway. Did he really see her that way?

"There are days I have my doubts," she finally managed to answer, as truthfully as she could.

"You shouldn't."

For several beats, Cassie could only manage to stand there, her mouth agape, staring at this Prince Charming of a man who seemed to know all the right words to say. The pinging of his cell phone finally broke the spell she'd fallen into unknowingly.

He dropped her hand to glance at the message and she could feel the loss of his warmth immediately.

"I'm sorry," he began. "My duty calls. Is there someone who can stay with you today? You mentioned a friend? They're welcome to come here."

Cassie shook her head. Zara was half a world away. "I'll be fine. Don't worry. I feel rested and refreshed. The good night's sleep served as a magical elixir. I truly appreciate it, Julian."

The smile returned. "I'm glad for it, Cassie. Thank you for saying so." He stole a glance at his watch, clearly reluctant. "I'm afraid now I'm due for that meeting. I should get going, it's in the financial district."

"Don't let me keep you." He'd done enough for her already.

"Are you going to be all right?" he asked, genuine concern infused in his tone.

Cassie had to suck in a breath, his words moving her in a way that nearly brought tears to her eyes. When was the last time someone had asked her that question and truly cared about the answer? Besides Zara, who was never around, she couldn't come up with a single answer.

"Please stay and enjoy the breakfast."

"Thank you. Again." How many times was that now?

He shrugged on a suit jacket, transforming into the quintessential businessman once more. "I've instructed the valet to call you a car service whenever you're ready to leave."

Was this man even real? He had an important early morning meeting yet had thought to order her room service and secure her transportation.

"Thank you." Ugh! Not again. But what else could she possibly say?

"Take your time, however."

No way. She couldn't say it yet again. Instead she would acknowledge the so-called elephant in the room. "I know I still owe you an answer," she stated as he walked to the door.

"*Si*. That you do."

She opened her mouth to say no, to just tell him once and for all that she couldn't do it, she couldn't take him up on his job offer though it was an opportunity she would have jumped at in her previous life, unable to believe her lucky stars. And to tell him to please not ask her why exactly she was turning him down.

But the words wouldn't form on her tongue and leave her mouth.

"I just need some more time to think about it," she said instead. "A few more hours."

He lifted an eyebrow, clearly surprised. Who could blame him?

"I look forward to hearing from you." But he didn't turn to leave. "There is one more thing, another matter that we probably should address, senorita."

Cassie could guess what he was referring to. Yet another proverbial elephant in the room. Sure enough, Julian walked over to the closed cabinet by the TV and removed something from its interior. The envelope from Carlos.

"This is still yours. To do with as you wish."

With that, he held it out it to her. "Read it, destroy it. It's up to you."

She should have known. Unlike his adopted cousin, Julian was the type to take his commitments and his promises seriously. Right or wrong, he'd been charged with delivering this envelope to her. And he'd made sure to do so.

Despite the ramifications of the gesture to her personally, she couldn't help but feel admiration that his adherence to his word was so strong and important to him.

Neither one of them said a word as he deposited the envelope into her hand. Cassie could only stare at the door as he shut it behind him.

"You weren't answering your phone last night."

Cassie pressed the speaker button on her cell as she entered her apartment two hours later, the blasted envelope still in her hand. Saints forgive her, but she'd taken Julian up on the offer to take her time in his suite. She didn't regret it. When would she be in such luxury again? Most likely the answer to that question was a resounding *never.*

"Hello?" Zara prompted from the other end of the line. And the other end of the world. Where was her globe-trotting friend again this time? She really couldn't recall. It wasn't pregnancy brain. Zara's schedule was just impossible to keep up with. One week she was in Paris, the next she'd jumped a plane to someplace like the Amazon. Being a world-class photographer made for an interesting life. A life she wouldn't dream of being able to experience.

Except that she was sitting on just such an opportunity herself right at this very moment. A chance to live an adventure for a short while, the way Zara led her whole life. A way she'd always admired and envied.

"I'm here," she finally answered, opening the windows after a long internal debate about whether the seaport smell would be preferable to the charred odor currently permeating her apartment. "Sorry, just getting in."

Cassie regretted the words as soon as she'd said them. The timing was so radically off her regular schedule that Zara was bound to ask about it, for answers she didn't quite know how to articulate just yet.

She was right.

"Oh? Where were you at this time in the morning?" Zara immediately asked. "Didn't you have to work late? And exactly why weren't you answering your phone anyway?"

Zara sounded nosy on the surface, but Cassie knew the myriad of questions originated from a place of love and concern. Her friend was the closest thing to family Cassie had. That she'd ever had, in fact.

She'd felt such a sense of lightening after speaking with Julian earlier. It would be good to get some of this off her chest some more and confide in the ever-wise Zara Shahada. Her firing was probably a good place to start.

"Well, see, it turns out I didn't have to work, in fact."

"Day off?"

"Several."

"Huh?"

"Martin fired me last night. You can probably guess the reason."

Zara released a torrent of curse words that

would have made any sailor proud, including references to Martin's parentage and lineage from swine species.

Despite herself, Cassie had to laugh at her friend's outraged reaction.

"I'm guessing you can't sue because he probably did it in a way to cover his behind."

"You'd be guessing right."

"I'm so sorry, Cassie. I never did trust that man."

"You've always been a great judge of character." Cassie admired that quality about her, wished she had some semblance of it herself. She might have guessed Carlos for the duplicitous fraud that he was.

"How are you feeling, beside that?" Zara asked. "Is everything okay with the baby?"

Cassie must have hesitated a tad too long. She could almost feel Zara's panic through the cell tower.

"What? What is it? Is something wrong with the baby?"

"No. Nothing like that," she quickly reassured. "It's just that I need so many things before he or she arrives. I don't know how

I'm going to afford any of it now. Newborns are not cheap."

Her gaze dropped to the envelope once more. She knew without a doubt that it held one of the choices that she might make about her future. But it was from a man who'd betrayed her and her unborn child. Who was she kidding? That fact alone made it no option at all.

"Oh, sweetie, I'll do anything I can to help," Zara was saying from the other end of the connection.

"Thank you, Zara," she answered simply. She wasn't anywhere near the point of accepting handouts from friends just yet. She knew firsthand how perilous that path could become.

"I hate that you're so upset. I can hop on a plane and be home in close to twenty-four hours. We'll figure this out together."

Tears began to sting behind her eyes. Zara's travel schedule was beyond tight. A disruption like the one she offered would throw her off for days and would definitely cost her a lot of money. Before Cassie knew it or could stop it, she found herself spilling the whole sordid story. Beginning with the fire, everything that had happened in between, and ending with her utter foolishness in actually considering Julian's job offer.

Zara was silent so long she thought maybe the connection had been lost. Finally, she heard her friend take a deep breath.

"Cassie?"

"Yes?"

"Have you taken up fiction writing and neglected to tell me? Because everything you just said sounds straight out of some kind of novel."

She sniffled before responding. "Yes. I mean, no. It's all true."

"Wow. That's a lot."

"You can say that again."

"Kind of impressive that you somehow lost your job then managed to find an infinitesimally better one all in the same day."

"Except I didn't really," Cassie argued.

"Why ever not? What exactly is holding you back?" Zara wanted to know. "If you want the job and need the money, just say yes."

Cassie squeezed her eyes shut. If only it

were that simple. Zara tended to see things as clear-cut, black or white. She'd gotten far in life that way. But it just wasn't the way Cassie was built.

"Things are a bit complicated, don't you think?"

"They don't have to be," her friend answered.

How could she be so blasé about the scenario Cassie had just laid out? She seemed to be trivializing her predicament. "For one, how am I supposed to tell Julian he's looking to hire a woman who's pregnant? Let alone pregnant with the baby of someone he's so close to?"

"Why do you need to tell him at all?"

The question gave Cassie pause. "Don't you think it's dishonest to keep that from him?"

"Why? In the US, you don't need to tell any employer about being pregnant until you're ready to ask for maternity leave, regardless of the circumstances."

She had a point there.

"You're not even far enough along," Zara continued. "And we're talking about a temporary position. From the sounds of it, you'll have fulfilled your obligation before anyone, including your prospective boss, even needs to know a thing."

Cassie hadn't even considered that. After all, it wasn't as if she was going to put her pregnant state on her CV. Julian was no different from any other manager she may have interviewed with. Of course, the wild card in this mess was Carlos. But Julian mentioned the two had nothing to do with each other's business dealings. She could simply tell Julian she didn't wish Carlos to know she worked for his so-called cousin.

Without giving herself a chance to change her mind, she ripped the envelope open and pulled out the documents inside. Despite fully expecting the contents and being 100 percent right about what she would find, she still felt the effect like a punch in her middle. The paperwork detailed the exact way she could access regular funds through an annuity account set up in her name. As well as a trust that would become liquid once the child turned sixteen.

All she had to do to put it in motion was sign on the line agreeing to never contact

Carlos at any time in the future. All contact had to be initiated by him.

Cassie couldn't help the crushing feeling of bitter disappointment and utter betrayal that burned through her chest. Not for herself, but for the child who would never know his or her father. On trembling legs, she walked over to the recycling chute, which led down to the building's main bin in the basement. She tossed the entire contents down into it with zero hesitation.

"You've gone silent." Zara jolted her back to the conversation, she'd almost forgotten the line was still live. "I hope that means you're seriously considering this Julian's offer," Zara added. "Honestly, Wells, you have nothing to lose."

Heaven help her, she really was thinking about it. Maybe she had been all this time and simply needed the kick of seeing in black and white the full reality of rejection by her baby's father.

As well as the gentle nudge from a dear and trusted friend. Zara was right. She had nothing to lose.

* * *

Julian glanced again for the umpteenth time at his phone screen. He'd been doing so all afternoon. Still nothing from Cassie. Should he reach out to her instead? Tell her that he needed to know one way or the other? One thing was for certain, he wasn't focusing at all on the meeting he was currently attending, simply going through the motions.

There was no reason for him to be this invested. Sure, he happened to be in a tight spot with a vacancy he needed filled sooner rather than later. But from the moment the idea had occurred to him, he'd wanted one person and one person only to fill the opening.

It made no logical sense. He'd be the first to admit it.

So why did his heart hammer in his chest when his screen finally lit up with an incoming call and her number appeared on caller ID? He stood with an apologetic nod to the other attendees. "Excuse me. I must take this."

Stepping outside of the conference room, he quickly made his way down the hall to a private office. His pulse raced through his veins. What if she said no?

"Is this a good time?" Cassie asked when he answered her call.

"Excellent," he lied. The truth was, he should still be in that meeting room, paying his full attention to the presentation that had been designed specifically for his benefit.

"I have an answer for you."

"I can't wait to hear it."

"I'd like to accept," he heard her say through the tiny speaker. Julian felt as if an invisible anvil had been lifted off his shoulders. Relief surged through his chest.

"If your offer still stands, I'd be honored to come work for you at the Paraiso resort." She seemed to blurt out the words, as if in a haste to get them out as soon as possible.

"Of course it does. The job is yours for the taking." He wished she were here in the room with him, wanted desperately to be able to see her face as she spoke. Something was off about her tone; her voice held a shakiness. As if she'd been crying and was now trying to pull herself together enough to get through this phone call.

Was she under some kind of duress? Questioning her decision already?

He shook off the thought. He was probably overanalyzing again, a habit he'd developed since Rosa. Questioning what he'd heard, wondering if there might be hidden messages under the spoken words.

"I can begin as soon as you need. I have no other commitments at the moment," Cassie added.

"That's excellent to hear, Cassie. You won't regret your choice."

She paused several moments before responding. "Thank you, Julian," she said simply, before the call went dead. But not before he could have sworn he heard her add another almost inaudible comment. He was certain he hadn't imagined it.

I hope and pray you're right.

CHAPTER FIVE

CASSIE STILL HADN'T convinced herself this whole experience wasn't some kind of dream she was having. Julian had booked her on a first-class flight to Palma de Mallorca within hours of her phone call accepting the job. From that point on, everything had seemed to happen in a blur. He'd sent her documents, secured her work papers and transferred an initial payment into her bank account. The man certainly worked fast.

Now, less than two weeks after that fateful call, she was about to disembark from her first international flight. She'd been apprehensive about flying, uncertain how the fumes and turbulence would affect her body in her current condition. But it had been a relaxing and enjoyable flight where she'd taken more than one nap. First-class seating definitely helped. By the time she landed, she felt rejuvenated and refreshed, ready to begin this adventure.

She made her way down to the terminal fully expecting to be greeted by a car service. But it was Julian himself who met her. Her heart did a small flip in her chest at the sight of him. She'd never seen him before in anything but a formal business suit. Now he was dressed much more casually, in pressed khakis and a sky blue shirt that accentuated the dark charcoal color of his eyes. His hair wasn't slicked back in the professional style of before, but fell in a soft wave over his forehead. She had to suck in a breath. That didn't bode well at all. She was here to do a job. This temporary stint was to advance her career and let her indulge in some unexpected travel. She had no business feeling any kind of pleasure or attraction upon seeing her boss again. That's all he was. Her boss.

"Cassie." He approached her with a wide smile, took her luggage from her hands. "I'm so glad you're finally here."

"Me too."

"How was your flight? Any issues?"

Cassie followed him out of the terminal

and to a waiting town car with a uniformed driver, who relieved Julian of her bags and tossed them in the trunk.

So, they were going to use a car service, after all. Yet he'd felt compelled to greet her himself upon her landing. Did she dare look too deep into that for some kind of hidden meaning? Cassie gave her head a brisk shake. Now she was being silly. Julian most likely had nothing but business on his mind and wanted to make sure his latest employee got here soundly.

His next words confirmed that suspicion.

"I'm afraid there is much work to be done. I figured we could discuss some of the more pressing to-dos during the drive. As soon as we arrive at the resort, you will have to hit the ground running—as you Americans would say."

"I'm anxious to get started."

"That's good."

She'd further read up on the resort and all its offerings. What a thrill to be involved in such a pioneering venture. Though it hadn't made much of a ripple in the States, Julian's all-female guest resort was garnering ample media attention in Europe since he'd recently announced it. Julian was being hailed as a daring and clever entrepreneur who had recognized a wide gap in the market. More and more, female travelers were looking to get away with other women on luxury trips focused on nothing but relaxation. Or they simply wanted to vacation solo and didn't want to have to deal with the unwanted male attention that seemed a magnet for any female by herself at a hotel.

The Paraiso Del Sol was set up just for such clientele. With over one hundred rooms, many of them overlooking the crystal blue water of the beach, and a majestic infinity pool, guests had ample access to sun and water.

"Tell me more about the resort," she prompted Julian as they pulled away and started their drive. The rather bumpy road threw off her equilibrium and threatened motion sickness, so she forced her gaze on the horizon. "What I wouldn't have read in the paperwork or brochures."

"We're still working out the kinks but there's plenty to do besides swim and snorkel."

Cassie was looking forward to the snorkeling part herself. She'd done it only once before when a classmate had invited her along for a family vacation to Cape Cod. The water outside her car window looked much calmer and definitely bluer than the Massachusetts coast. Though she was guessing it would be too cold currently. Hopefully, she'd get a chance to snorkel before her assignment ended in a few weeks. Thinking about leaving already caused a dull ache of disappointment. She had to remind herself none of this was permanent. She just recently accepted that it was really happening.

Julian continued, "There are spa packages which offer everything from beauty services to massage to aromatherapy. But there's also plenty of adventure to be had. We have scuba lessons and licensed scuba instructors, daily yoga and fitness classes, and outings to the city and attractions nearby."

And she was officially in charge of making sure it all fell into place before opening and then ran smoothly once their first guests arrived. As well as working with a marketing team to get word out about the resort to a worldwide customer base. On top of all that, she'd be tasked with interviewing and hiring necessary staff. Julian had been generous with her salary but there was no doubt she would earn every penny of it.

Her stomach churned with apprehension as she thought of the sheer magnitude of responsibility. Under normal circumstances, she'd be much more confident in herself and her abilities. But there was more to consider now. Her stamina seemed to be diminishing more and more with each passing day.

"You've gone quiet suddenly. Is everything all right?" Julian asked in the seat next to her.

Before she could answer, the car hit some type of ditch in the road and the driver turned the wheel so suddenly, she slid across the seat. Straight into Julian's lap. His arms immediately went protectively around her shoulders.

For one horrified instant, she wondered exactly how long she might remain there in his arms, held tightly against him and his solid strength. When his cologne tickled her nostrils, she realized with a jolt that she'd missed the now familiar scent of him.

"Are you all right, *bella*?"

The endearment threw her off for a moment; he'd never referred to her in that way before. Again, nothing to read into, she was certain. Julian was simply more at home in his native environment and speaking much more informally and comfortably.

Finally, she managed to pull away and shifted back to her side of the back seat. Was it her imagination, or had Julian's arms held her an instant longer than necessary? Just a tad tighter than the situation might have called for?

"I'm fine. Guess I should be wearing a seat belt." In the back of her mind, she chastised herself for not doing so to begin with. She was with child, after all.

"The road can be a little bumpy this stretch of the ride," Julian offered before they fell into an awkward silence. Cassie reached for the safety belt over her shoulder and fastened it into place.

"I was just admiring the view." She answered his earlier question, just to start up some sort of conversation again. "It really is breathtaking." Though it wasn't a completely honest reply, her words were plaintively true.

The striking blue hue of the water against a cloudy crystal blue sky accented with majestic mountains looked like a scene out of a masterpiece painting.

Julian had given her a huge opportunity in offering her this job, in all manner of ways. She vowed to make the most of it. For both her sake and her child's. The demanding position would take discipline and hard work and probably all her energy for the next several weeks. On top of that, she had to take care of herself and make sure the baby she carried remained healthy and thriving.

She had her work cut out for her. She couldn't afford to stumble or be distracted in any way.

And she absolutely could not complicate things further by indulging in any kind of attraction she had to her boss.

About an hour later, they pulled up to a long circular driveway leading to a Spanish villa–style structure overlooking a long expanse of beach. It was hard to decide which was the clearer blue, the sky or the water.

She did a double take when Julian led her to

what he said would be her accommodations during her assignment. She thought maybe she'd misheard him when he opened the door and stepped aside to let her in the room.

"Uh. This is where I'll be staying, then?"

He nodded. "Unless you'd prefer something else. Is it not to your liking?"

He had to be kidding. Who in their right mind would find this place not to their liking?

"I figured you'd like the view." He motioned toward the large sliding glass doors that lead out to a balcony overlooking the ocean. He'd figured right. The scene before her was breathtaking.

"It's absolutely stunning." Suddenly a lump of emotion she couldn't quite place formed at the base of her throat. A week ago, she wouldn't have dreamed she'd be living in a Spanish villa on Mallorca's coast in a room overlooking the crystal blue waters of the Spanish Mediterranean. She turned to Julian. "Thank you, Julian. Truly. I don't know what to say."

"I'm glad you like it, senorita," He waited a beat as if studying her. "You're very welcome."

"You didn't have to give me such an extravagant suite." It would have been much more prudent for him to keep the suite unused and in pristine condition for the arrival of their first guests.

"Nonsense, I have to make sure my most valued employee is productive and comfortable."

Of course, that was his only motivation behind the decision to give her such a room. She was being foolish to feel at all touched by the gesture. "Still, this has to be one of the deluxe rooms. You could have left it untouched."

He winked at her with a wide smile. "I'm glad you think so, but this isn't a deluxe room. Those aren't quite ready yet."

That took her for a turn. If a posh decorated room with a view of the majestic cliffs and ocean wasn't a deluxe, she couldn't wait to see what one was. Julian must have read her thoughts. "I'll be sure to take you to one real soon. Now, I'll leave you to freshen up. Meet me on the first floor as soon as you're ready."

For what exactly? "Ready?"

"You're about to start your first training session."

Cassie clapped her hands in front of her chest. "Good. I'm happy to hit the ground running. The sooner I start, the better." Though she was tired and hungry, Cassie absolutely meant what she said. Her adrenaline and excitement made for potent motivators. She couldn't wait to start exploring the resort and learning her responsibilities.

"Happy to hear it," Julian said. "But it's not all work and no play here. I think you'll find this to be one of the more enjoyable parts of the job."

Well, that statement certainly had her intrigued. "I will?"

He nodded with a mischievous smile. "Especially if you're hungry."

In fact, she was famished. She hadn't wanted to let on and inconvenience Julian in any way, but her first order of business once he left her was to try to scrummage around the kitchen for a bite to eat. Now it appeared he had other plans. She wasn't sure how much longer her roiling stomach could hold out, however.

"I wouldn't turn down a bite or two. Now that you mention it."

"Excellent, I'll wait for you downstairs, then. Our new chef is working on some prospective dishes for the menu. She asked us to be her taste testers. I realize that duty wasn't explicitly on your job description but I'm hoping you'll grant us some leeway."

"Of course I will. I can't wait to try her dishes," Cassie responded, somewhat concerned. What kind of feedback would she be able to offer? It wasn't as if she was any kind of foodie or had been exposed to international cuisine much throughout her lifetime. "Though I'm afraid I don't have a terribly discerning palate. I'm not sure how much of a help I might be."

He leaned toward her, his voice lowered to a false whisper. "I wouldn't fret. You just need to let her know if you like the dish or not. Between you and me, I think it might be her way of welcoming you on board," he said conspiratorially.

"That's so very kind. I can't wait to meet her."

"Come down when you're ready, *bella*. And we'll get started."

There was that term again. Cassie couldn't

seem to help the sensation of warmth that washed over her skin whenever he referred to her with the endearment. Though surely Julian couldn't really mean anything by it. No doubt he uttered the word without thinking, most likely a cultural or language thing. Nothing more.

"I'll be there as soon as I can. I'm really looking forward to it."

He turned to leave and Cassie had to fight an urge to thank him yet again, in a replay of that morning in the Harbor Hotel in Boston. The words weren't adequate anyway. Looking around the room once more and glancing at the majestic scene outside, she knew she wouldn't be able to fully communicate just how much it was all coming to mean to her.

Cassie must really think him a heartless ogre, Julian thought as he left her room and made his way downstairs.

Of course he was going to give her time to freshen up and have a meal after the day of travel she'd had. It made him wonder how many people in her life had refused to give her even the smallest considerations. Or how often in life she'd put herself behind others' needs and expectations.

Well, she would soon learn that as his resort manager her needs would take a back seat to no one. Particularly not his own. This place was geared toward women, after all. That meant her opinion and satisfaction took prevalence over his. Essentially, she was going to be his right-hand point person for the next several weeks. That meant that for all intents and purposes, she was no less than an equal partner.

Their first mutual decision as such would be to help Safina, his head chef, determine which dishes she would focus on for the main restaurant's menu options.

When she appeared in the lobby about twenty minutes later, Cassie looked refreshed and ready to begin. She'd changed into a loose-fitting cotton dress with a skirt that ended just above her knees. She really did have shapely legs. Not that he should be noticing that kind of thing. As she approached, the delicate scent of rose floated in the air. She'd put her hair up in some type of loose bun on the top of her head. The style accented the delicate shape of her face and gave her a look that was somehow elegant yet casual.

The woman looked completely in place here at the Paraiso. The sight of her eradicated any doubt he may have still held on to about his choice. He'd absolutely chosen wisely.

Cassie looked like exactly the type of manager who should be running this kind of resort. That thought gave him pause. Their understanding originally was that she stay and work for him for only a month. He had a suspicion he was going to want to revisit that with her before those weeks were up.

"I'm ready to go taste," she told him with a cheerful wave when she reached his side.

He returned her smile with one of his and offered her his elbow to lead her outside.

"We're going outdoors for this?" she asked.

"Figured you'd like the air after being cooped up in an airplane for so long," he explained, leading her down the man-made stone steps that brought them down to the beach.

She gave his elbow a slight squeeze. The contact had an electric current shooting up his arm. What was wrong with him? Noticing the way her dress complemented her figure and shapely legs. Feeling physical sensations at the mere touch of her hand. Noting the way she smelled. It was all completely unacceptable. He'd been single for too long. That had to be his issue. When was the last time he'd escorted a woman by the arm down the beach?

He immediately shoved away the question as memories began to assault his mind. Memories much better left unvisited. Memories that had almost torn him to shreds two short years ago.

"Thank you, Julian," Cassie added. "That was very considerate of you."

"It was Safina's idea," he answered, a bit more gruffly than he'd intended. Cassie loosened her grip on him ever so slightly at his tone.

In moments, they'd reached the canvas tent where Safina had set up a long buffet table that held several silver trays with burners underneath. She wore an authentic chef's hat as she greeted them both with warm hugs.

After the initial introductions, Safina presented them with an appetizer plate of olives and gourmet cheeses along with crusty bread.

"This is *pane de sal*," the chef informed Cassie. "Traditional Spanish bread prepared with a dash of salt." She added some minor details about preparation.

Julian watched as Cassie sampled several bites of each. She closed her eyes after swallowing, an expression of sheer pleasure on her face. Julian found he had to look away out toward the ocean and count a few beats.

"You absolutely have to include this as an appetizer option, Safina," she said breathlessly.

The next dish was fresh fish stew. "I've prepared this using cod with clam juice, lemon and a rich vegetable broth. Along with fresh herbs and spices."

Once again, Cassie's expression said all that was needed. She was clearly impressed with the soup.

"Safina, I have to tell you your presentation is downright entertaining," she said, after taking several more spoonfuls.

The other woman beamed at the compliment. "Thank you. I've dreamed of being one of those celebrity chefs on television," Safina said with a friendly smile in response. The two women were definitely hitting it off.

Cassie had an affable and pleasant personality that seemed to make most people around her feel comfortable and familiar. He had no doubt that quality would be a hit with the resort clientele. He had half a mind to ask her to pose for marketing brochures on top of her regular duties.

That same feeling from earlier settled through his bones again. Cassie belonged here. In every sense. Now that she was on the resort, Julian was having problems imagining the place without her. As fanciful as it sounded, the feeling was powerful and resounding.

And it totally threw him off balance. In fact, her mere presence did.

Dios! He had to get a grip. Earlier, he'd called her *bella*. More than once. The word had just seemed to naturally roll off his tongue when he was talking to her. Then he'd touched her and held her in the back seat of the car. But one thing was absolutely certain: he couldn't use words of endearment for her or touch her again in any way. She was an employee who worked for him. That alone made his words and actions inappropriate.

He couldn't allow himself to slip up so badly again. Cassie deserved better than what he had to offer.

CHAPTER SIX

CASSIE COULD HARDLY believe she was getting paid for this.

An explosion of wonder was occurring in her mouth and on her tongue. Taste after taste of delicious food served in a wondrous beach-side setting wasn't a scene she would have foreseen in her future. Yet, here she was.

This was as close to a luxurious vacation as she'd ever come. Yet somehow, she'd be compensated handsomely for it. It had been a while since Lady Luck had smiled on her. But she certainly seemed to have come through this time.

"Well, that's about it for me," Safina said after clearing their latest tapas plate. She gestured to the two chairs sitting at the end of the buffet table. "Why don't you two sit down and eat what's left of the food? A busboy is due down soon to clear all this up."

"Why don't you join us, Safina?" Cassie

asked without thinking, not that she thought Julian would have an issue with her invitation. But perhaps she should have at least run it by him. She was becoming too comfortable her first afternoon on the island.

Moot point because the other woman answered that she was much too busy with a food shipment coming in from the mainland. "Plus, I've been having tiny tasting bites all day and they've added up," the chef admitted, patting her stomach with a hearty chuckle. She left after that, leaving her and Julian with the remaining food.

"Let's move on to the fresh oysters, *si*?" he asked her after pushing her chair in.

Cassie's stomach did a dip. Oysters were usually consumed raw. Raw shellfish was an absolute no-no for a woman who was expecting. Trying one was out of the question. "I'm not much of a raw food connoisseur," she hedged, hoping he wouldn't insist.

"Ah, but these are grilled over an open flame," Julian countered, picking one up off the plate. "She's grilled them right in the half shell. And I see she's added some pimiento and a tangy fish sauce."

It still didn't sound terribly appetizing. Though grilled oysters weren't prohibited, Cassie wasn't exactly in any kind of rush to have one. What she knew of oysters was that they were slimy and slid down your throat. Not a sensation she savored under normal conditions let alone while expecting. Her reluctance must have shown on her face given Julian's next words. "It's completely up to you, of course. But may I share a secret with you?"

"An oyster secret? Sure. Shoot."

"The secret to eating them, no matter how they're served, is to not watch."

Cassie blinked. "Not watch?"

He nodded. "Precisely. Close your eyes as you put the oyster into your mouth, don't open them again until after you've swallowed."

"Uh…"

"Here, let me show you," Julian said before proceeding to demonstrate exactly what he'd described. "You only need your sense of taste. And these taste delicious."

Why not try? Cassie thought. She was completely out of her normal environment in so many ways. What was one more thing to try?

Gingerly, she picked up one of the half shells, closed her eyes and opened her lips. Only to promptly miss her mouth.

Oyster juice splashed over her chin and down her chest. She heard Julian chuckle right as she snapped her eyes open. He quickly reached for a napkin and wiped off the offending liquid before it had a chance to reach the fabric of her chest. But not before the gesture had her breath catching in her throat.

When she looked up, any hint of amusement had left his eyes. Shadows of heat darkened their depths. Cassie had to remind herself to breathe.

She watched in silent anticipation as he lifted the last grilled oyster off the plate. "Allow me, *por favor*," he said as he gently lifted her chin with his forefinger. "Close your eyes for me." His voice sounded like a caress, and his hand felt like silk against the bare skin of her chin.

Heat curled through her core. Her pulse pounded underneath her skin. Before she could think, she was following his instructions. She parted her lips slowly, her breath coming out in tiny, quick gasps. The air around them seemed to suddenly grow quiet, only the soft laps of the gentle waves provided any background noise. She felt the delicacy on her tongue for the barest of an instant before she somehow managed to swallow it, all the while keeping her eyes shut.

"What do you think?" Julian was asking.

Think? Who could think? Slowly she opened her eyes to face him squarely. His intense gaze on her face made her heart do a dance.

"It's delicious," she managed after a long pause where neither one of them so much as moved. "But I don't think I'll be having it again." She stood quickly, not certain if her legs would even hold her. Every muscle in her body felt like gelatin. "I think I'll start piling some of these dishes. Make the cleanup easier for the—"

But she didn't get a chance to finish. Safina stood only a few feet away, her mouth agape, staring at them. The look of sheer surprise on her face couldn't have made it clearer just how much she'd witnessed.

The other woman slowly cleared her throat.

"I…uh…forgot my chef's hat." She pointed to the table.

Cassie wanted to sink into the ground. She'd so wanted the staff to like and respect her, starting with the affable head chef she'd met first. Instead, she'd been caught being hand-fed by the boss. What must Safina think of her?

She didn't even want to guess. It made little sense, but though they'd just met, Cassie had already begun to feel a fondness for the other woman. Now her perception of Cassie would be unduly colored at the very least.

What a ridiculous situation to put herself in. And on her first afternoon here, no less. This appeared to be her year to make terrible decisions.

She couldn't look Safina or Julian in the eye as she excused herself before somehow managing to walk away.

For the next forty-eight hours Cassie made sure to focus solely on the momentous undertaking before her in getting the resort and its staff fully prepared for the grand opening. She studied blueprints, walked the property, analyzed countless CVs—no easy task given the language barrier—and spent time in the kitchen familiarizing herself with the dining protocols. To her credit, Safina made no mention of what she'd witnessed on the beach the other day nor so much as betrayed any sign that she'd been privy to such a private moment. Still, she must have come to some kind of conclusion about what was going on between Cassie and their mutual boss. The thought that the other woman was no doubt speculating on that score brought a flush to her cheeks. It was truly mortifying.

And what exactly was going on between them?

Darned if she knew. All she knew was that she couldn't deny her attraction to him. She'd woken up last night in the middle of a rather heated dream. In her sleep, the scene from the beach played out very differently after he'd fed her the oyster. For one, they hadn't been interrupted. And Cassie, rather than walking away, had ended up in Julian's lap.

She'd bolted awake, hot, clammy and with her pulse racing.

Up until that telling dream, she'd been trying to convince herself that there was nothing to concern herself with. Julian was a very handsome man. The days in his native land had deepened the tanned color of his skin. She could see exactly how he was maintaining that toned physique. Julian was involved with every facet of the resort operations, including maintenance and a lot of the labor intensive tasks. He wasn't afraid to get his hands dirty.

All of which made trying to avoid the man nearly impossible. He seemed to be everywhere.

Heaven help her, she found that characteristic alluring, as well. If only she'd met him a few months ago. Before that fateful night in Boston when the bachelor party had stumbled in. But of course, that made no sense. The turn her life had taken that night was the only reason she'd even met Julian.

A twinge of guilt twisted her insides that Julian had no idea about any of it. But there was nothing for that now. What was she supposed to do? Sit him down and come clean? She could only imagine his reaction. And where would that leave them both? She didn't think he would be annoyed enough to fire her, but the awkwardness resulting from the revelation would be too much to bear. She had enough on her mind.

Maybe it had just been her imagination or the excitement of her new life, but she could have sworn she felt the slightest ruffle of movement in her belly late in the evening yesterday. Though she knew it was much too early to feel any kind of kicking, in her heart, she had no doubt it was the baby reminding her that they were in there. Waiting to reveal themselves. The thought had made her heady with excitement and nearly cripplingly anxious at the same time.

As if she forgot for even one moment about the little one's pending arrival in a few months time.

She just had to hold it together and do a good job here. Doing so would go a long way toward ensuring a secure future for her child, which she desperately wanted to provide. The possibility of failure in that regard scared her witless. No matter what happened, she couldn't become a mother like the one who'd raised her. If you could call that raising a child. No, Marion had been much too self-absorbed, much too erratic and much too irresponsible to qualify as any kind of real parent.

Her mother had never passed on an opportunity to remind Cassie that she hadn't been planned and wasn't wanted. Being tossed from foster home to foster home had cemented the point over the years.

By contrast, though Cassie's pregnancy might not have been timed as she had hoped, every fiber of her being already loved this baby and wanted it desperately.

Cassie vowed daily to never let him or her forget it. She wasn't going to let anything get in the way of that goal. Least of all her taboo attraction to a man who happened to be so completely off-limits.

Cassie was definitely avoiding him.

He would have to be a fool not to see it. Not that he could blame her. Hadn't he sworn that he would be more professional when it came to her? That was right before he'd nearly seduced her on the beach in front of his head chef.

Julian sighed and rubbed a hand down his face. Leaning over the railing of his sailboat, he gazed at the star-filled Mallorcan sky above and uttered a small curse. He had to do better. There was no room in his life for anything romantic. He simply wasn't ready yet. Not after the fiasco with Rosa, the way she'd humiliated him.

Not to mention, the resort opening took precedence over his wayward hormones. He had to be sure Cassie felt comfortable enough around him to do her job. He had no assurance that she did. Whatever this spark was between them, it had to be throwing both of them off-balance. Heaven knew, he was having trouble focusing. And he had too much to do. As did she. So, he had no choice but to figure out how to stop his wayward thoughts when it came to Cassie.

It wasn't going to be easy. They had a lot to get done together, starting tomorrow when he would take her sailing to show her the various snorkeling spots their guests would have access to.

He was a businessman, a professional. He

just had to keep reminding himself of that. And he would, Julian vowed. Even as he couldn't stop thinking about her.

CHAPTER SEVEN

As FAR AS mornings went, they couldn't have asked for a more perfect one for a day spent sailing around the bay. The sun was bright and the sky was clear; the sea a calm and smooth blanket of glittery blue. It was too cold to snorkel just yet, but he'd at least be able to show Cassie some of the ideal locations for their guests to participate in the activity.

Julian watched now as she approached from the wooden dock wearing a large straw hat and silky sundress held up with thin straps. When she neared, he helped her board the midsize cruiser he'd purchased for snorkeling excursions.

He'd vowed just yesterday to try and keep his distance, at least mentally when it came to her. But the sight of her brought home just how difficult that would be. She'd acquired some color during her short time on the island and now sported just enough of a tan that it accented her dark eyes and highlighted the black hue of her hair. The sundress was a bright red color that perfectly suited her overall coloring. She was a stunning woman. He had no doubt that many men over the years had noticed it. In fact, he had to wonder why there was no man in her life currently. Maybe her fierce need to guard her privacy was the result of a recent bad breakup. The theory would explain a lot.

Julian groaned internally. He sincerely hoped his cousin had played no part in that likely scenario.

She greeted him with a wide smile as she held up a canvas parcel bag once she was on board. "Safina made us some sandwiches."

"They won't go to waste."

Moments later, they were drifting off on the open water toward a few of the many coves surrounding the island. Julian began pointing out the spots tourists had as options if they wanted to spend a couple hours snorkeling or simply enjoy an extended swim in Mediterranean waters.

"This is so breathtakingly beautiful, Julian.

Your guests will love these adventures. I have no doubt about it. And I'll make sure that's all communicated fully when I meet with the marketing team."

"Correction, *bella*." He tapped her nose, fully aware that he'd once again used the endearment he swore countless times not to use. "They'll be *our* guests."

Something darkened behind her eyes and she quickly looked away off toward the horizon.

Julian sailed them around another hour or so before removing the pair of binoculars he'd worn around his neck and handing them to her. Then he gently took her by the shoulders to adjust her position. A sensation of warmth spread from the palms of his hands where his skin met hers. As much as he knew that he should stop touching her immediately, he couldn't seem to bring himself to do so.

"Here," he said and brought up the binoculars to her eyes. "You can see the limestone mountains up close."

She sucked in a breath as she peered through the lenses. "They're so beautiful. This entire spot is just lovely."

"Then this is the spot we'll stop to anchor and enjoy our lunch."

They ate mostly in silence, with some small talk about the beauty of the island and whether it was what she'd expected.

"Why'd you choose this spot to open your resort anyway?" she asked between bites of her sandwich.

He shrugged. "My family owns a good amount of land along the coast. The responsibility of determining what to do with it fell to me after my father passed." He looked out toward the distance, thinking about how much his late father loved this scene. How often they would come out here as children to spend the day snorkeling and swimming.

It had been such a simple time for him.

"Tell me about him," Cassie prompted, her voice gentle and urging.

Thoughts of his father were always bittersweet and filled him with a melancholy sadness. But he found himself glad for the opportunity to talk about him with Cassie. He wanted her to know what kind of man he'd been. Before he could begin, he cleared his throat to remove the emotion that choked him.

"My father was an amazing man. He made his way here by himself when he was barely a teen, from the slums of Barcelona. Through hard work and sheer determination, he managed to buy valuable land and opened several businesses. Once established, he devoted his entire self to being a good father and husband. We were all devastated when we lost him."

He didn't want to bring Carlos up again to her. So he didn't bother to add details about how his adopted cousin had gone from badly misbehaved teen to a downright rebellious one after his father's passing. His behavior had added yet more drama and pain to an already grieving family. Nor would Julian tell her about all the times he'd bailed Carlos out over the years, both literally and figuratively.

"With you left as the only one to try and fill his shoes," Cassie supplied, her tone full of tenderness and concern.

Julian scoffed at that. "Not possible. No one could fill his shoes."

"From where I'm standing, I'd say you did pretty well. Everything I've read so far tells me you grew the family business several fold."

The touch of admiration in her voice had him ridiculously pleased. How silly of him to be so moved by her compliment.

He forced his attention back to Cassie's original question about the resort location. "Anyway, the whole area is becoming highly commercialized. I held out as long as I could to keep it untouched. But it was only a matter of time given the growth surrounding it. That's why I wanted to find a way to differentiate what we had to offer."

"Hence, the exclusively female aspect."

"Precisely," Julian answered.

"I hope I get to go snorkeling before I leave," Cassie ventured after several silent beats.

"An avid snorkeler, are you?"

She rolled her eyes and chuckled. "Hardly. I've only been once. And I loved it. So much wonder to see and behold under the ocean."

"Then why didn't you do it again?"

She looked off into the distance toward the horizon. "I only had the one chance. A friend of mine invited me along on a family trip."

"That's too bad. And another opportunity never happened to come along?"

She shrugged slightly. "Yes and no. One of the families I was placed with mentioned heading to Florida every summer to visit their grandparents who lived there. An annual fishing slash boating trip was one of the main events. I was really looking forward to going." She released a deep sigh. "It never happened."

"Why not?"

"My mother showed up early that spring. Wanted me back. One of the many times she'd pulled that on me. By the time summer rolled around, she'd convinced the court she was clean and sober and ready to be a mother. Needless to say, it didn't last. And I never saw that particular foster family again."

Julian never doubted how fortunate he'd been with all that he'd been given in life. But hearing Cassie's story made him realize just how blessed he'd been to have had two devoted and loving parents. Even if he'd lost one of them much too soon.

Now he wanted nothing more than to be able to pull Cassie into his arms and soothe

the sadness out of her. Then he wanted to indulge in the kiss he'd been thinking of for so long. He wanted to kiss her until she forgot about the sadness altogether and all she could think about was the taste of him, the feel of him.

He made himself push the selfish, useless thought aside.

Cassie continued after another wistful sigh, "That was one of the first times I swore that I'd be a completely different kind of mo—"

Before she could finish, a gust of wind blew Cassie's hat askew and slightly pitched the boat.

Suddenly, the color drained from her face and she smacked a palm over her lips. The area beneath her eyes rapidly grew green.

"Are you all right?"

She scrambled from her seated position, her hand still clamped tight around her mouth.

"I'm fine," she said in a muffled voice. "I guess I just ate a little too quickly. Excuse me." With that, she swiftly strode to the stairway leading below deck.

Julian polished off the rest of his lunch and figured he'd better put hers away. It was probably past time they started back to the dock anyway. Lifting anchor, he started turning the boat around.

He began to grow concerned when Cassie hadn't returned several minutes later. Funny, she'd shown no sign of seasickness the whole morning and early afternoon. And the breeze had noticeably picked up but it would hardly be considered blustering wind. Just enough to gently sway the boat from side to side. In fact, he for one found it rather soothing. Then again, he'd grown up sailing boats around this island. But Cassie was from Boston. She lived near the harbor. Surely, she'd been aboard a boat before and on choppier water than this.

Maybe their conversation had gotten too intense.

He was about to drop anchor once more to go check on her when she reappeared above deck. Definitely on wobbly legs.

"Are you feeling any better?" he asked. She certainly didn't look it. Somehow, she'd grown even paler. The circles under her eyes were deeper and darker.

"If it's all the same with you, I'd like to

head back to dry land now. I'm going to go lie down in the meantime."

It was clear she was suffering a sudden, severe bout of seasickness. So why wouldn't she just say so?

"Of course," he assured her. But she'd already turned to go back below.

CHAPTER EIGHT

SO THAT WAS what full-blown morning sickness felt like. She'd been on much choppier water in the past and she'd been fine. What she'd experienced back there, the queasiness, the nausea, the punishing urge to eliminate the piece of toast she'd had for breakfast and the small amount of lunch she'd managed to eat, was unlike anything she'd been dealt so far. Or perhaps it was a combination of morning sickness and motion sickness altogether.

All she knew was it had nearly knocked her off her feet.

Cassie rushed back to her suite as soon as they docked at the island. Luckily, Julian wasn't asking too many questions. "You'll find your sea legs soon enough," he assured her as she ran down the wooden pathway toward the beach.

"I'll come check on you later," he added, yelling at her retreating back.

Cassie could barely make out his words in her rush to get away. She'd already been physically ill once, she didn't want him to witness the next time. And it was clear there'd be a next time.

Luckily the feeling seemed to be subsiding. Though it had come at a very inopportune time. Julian had been trying to show her the best places to snorkel. She'd be lucky if she retained any of it. If not, she'd be behind in at least one of her duties. After a quick, refreshing nap, she jumped in the shower to clean up and try to regain some semblance of normalcy.

By the time she left the shower, the nausea seemed to be only a lingering aftereffect. Thank heavens. She had no hope of functioning if this was going to be a recurring thing. She might have to consider making a trip in to see a doctor at the local medical clinic to ask about some of her options.

Quickly toweling off and getting dressed in a comfortable smock dress, she flung open her door to make her way back down to the lobby.

Only to run into Julian mid-knock. Literally. They collided with a heavy thud.

"Oomph."

Panic rushed through her veins when she lost her footing and began to topple backward. *The baby.*

Suddenly, a set of strong arms wrapped around her midsection. "Whoa. Careful."

Cassie felt the relief clear to her toes as he steadied her on her feet. His arms were still wrapped tight around her as she took her time to regain her breath.

"Are you all right?" he asked above her head.

"I—I think so."

"Still having trouble balancing?"

"Maybe just a little."

Julian made no move to release her. Cassie found she wasn't quite ready to pull away yet either. She felt safe in his arms, protected. Like she could finally let go and breathe. The now familiar scent of spicy cologne and sea air combined with his soothing warmth all enveloped her like a protective cocoon.

She realized what she hadn't been willing to face up until now. She felt safe with Julian.

And heaven help her, she was beginning to develop feelings for him. Complicated beyond all reason, but she'd be a fool to deny it any longer. Beyond mere attraction, and there was certainly plenty of that, she genuinely felt an affection for the man that she hadn't seen coming. Not until it was too late. She wasn't prepared.

"Are you sure you're simply suffering from seasickness?" he asked. "Maybe we should have Safina or one of the other staff members take you to the medical building in town." His grip on her seemed to grow slightly tighter. Still, she made no move to pull away.

Cassie's mouth went dry. This was it. She had to tell him the truth. There was no easy way, best to just blurt it out and let all the pieces fall where they may. She could only hope he would understand why she'd kept it from him all this time. Cassie swallowed past the lump in her throat and struggled to form the words.

"Julian, I need to—"

She felt more than saw or heard the approach of another person down the hallway. They weren't alone any longer. Looking past

Julian's shoulder, she found a middle-aged woman standing several feet away. Dressed in an elegant pantsuit with large gold hoops, she had dark wavy hair and eyes that looked rather familiar. Though Cassie couldn't quite place how.

Cassie didn't know whether to be relieved or groan in frustration at the interruption. She didn't know how she would ever work up the nerve again to tell Julian about the pregnancy.

The woman looked like exactly the type of clientele they wanted to attract to a resort such as this one. But guests weren't due to arrive for several more weeks. Had Julian invited some earlier guests as test subjects? He should have told her if that was the case.

"Hola," the woman said with a small wave, her smile remaining in place.

Against her chest Julian released a deep sigh and slowly removed his arms from around her. He gave her a small wink before turning around to meet the new arrival. *"Buenos días, Madre."*

Julian wanted desperately to linger with Cassie to make sure she was feeling better.

But it appeared their conversation would have to wait. Still, he had to ask her once more. "Are you sure you're all right now?"

She gave him a reassuring nod, though she still hadn't taken her eyes off his mother.

"Aren't you going to introduce us?" Maria asked, with a knowing smile. He could just guess what she was thinking after walking in on them in what could only be described as an embrace. Not that it was anything romantic. But this wasn't exactly the time to try and clarify that now, was it?

He took Cassie gently by the elbow and led her to where his mother stood.

"This is Cassie, Mother. She's my new resort manager."

Maria quirked an eyebrow as she held her hand out. "Manager, huh? I see." Her tone said she didn't see at all. Julian stifled a curse. He was not looking forward to the conversation his mother would insist on having later. And what was he going to say? That it wasn't what it looked like? Not like he could effectively explain. He wasn't exactly sure how to explain it to himself. All he knew was that he'd grown increasingly concerned about Cassie since she'd run off after disembarking earlier this afternoon. As the minutes had ticked by and she still hadn't shown up back to work, he felt an overwhelming urge to go make sure she was all right. When was the last time he'd felt such angst over an employee's health?

The answer was *never*.

He'd grown to care about her. A fact he had to face. And he cared about her in a way that was much more loaded than a boss-employee relationship. He hadn't even seen it coming. It was exactly what he'd been trying to avoid and somehow he'd missed its progression altogether. So how could he have stopped it?

Right now, there was a more pressing matter to deal with. His mother.

What was she doing here anyway?

He asked her just that in Spanish, at the risk of being rude to Cassie, though not in those exact words.

The two women hadn't taken their eyes off each other. Both continued smiling.

"I came to see my oldest son," his mother replied in English. "As I was tired of waiting for an invite."

Julian sighed. "We're not quite ready for guests. You would have been our first invite as soon as we were," he reassured her.

His mother's smile faded a little. "I'm more than a mere guest though, aren't I?"

Finally, she tore her gaze away from Cassie and stepped over to give him a loving caress against his cheek. "Besides, I missed you, *mi niño.*"

"I missed you too, Mother. I'm simply concerned that we may not have the right accommodations for you, as unprepared as we are."

"And this is why I didn't announce my arrival." She patted his cheek before dropping her hand back to her side. "I guessed you would try to dissuade me."

She was right on that score. As much as he loved and adored his mother, Julian didn't have the time or the mental energy to deal with her right now, not with everything on his plate.

Cassie cleared her throat next to them. When she spoke, he was surprised at how firm and steady her voice sounded. Hopefully, she truly was feeling better. After all, most people fell into a shaky stutter in Maria's presence under the best of circumstances. She seemed to have that kind of effect on others. Damned if he could explain why.

"I'll go see about a room for you," Cassie said.

His mother turned her observant eyes in Cassie's direction. "Why, thank you, dear. I hope it won't be too much trouble for you."

Cassie shook her head. "No trouble at all, Senora Santigo."

Maria waved an expertly manicured hand dismissively in the air. "You must call me Maria. *Por favor.*"

Cassie returned her smile. "Of course. Thank you. I'll go see about the room, then."

"I would suggest seven-one-seven," he said to her retreating back. "In the Del Sol building. The key card is behind the lobby desk. You will need to program it."

Cassie gave him a nod over her shoulder and continued walking.

"Your manager, huh?" his mother asked before Cassie was completely out of earshot.

Julian pinched the bridge of his nose. She wasn't going to give him a chance to delay this at all, was she?

"Yes, Madre. That is all."

Maria lifted a shoulder. "If you say so, *mi niño*."

"Yes. And she's doing an excellent job so far despite having just started. I found her in America. Boston to be precise." He didn't want to get into the details behind their meeting. "So please stop looking at me like that."

Maria clasped a hand to her chest in a gesture of innocence but the twinkle in her eye gave her away. "Like what?"

"Like you're impatient for me to 'spill the beans,' as the Americans would say. There are no beans to spill."

"So, you're saying appearances can be deceiving? That I shouldn't believe what I saw with my own eyes as I walked into this hallway."

"That is precisely what I'm saying, Mother. I'd like to please just drop the whole thing."

Maria gave him an affectionate smile, cupped his cheek once more. "Of course, dear. I don't want to upset you. I just worry about you still. You haven't been the same since…"

Julian took her hesitancy as a chance to

interrupt her. "I know you do, Mother. But there's no need. I've moved on. Just as Rosa has."

His mother waited a beat, clearly debating whether to say more. But luckily, she dropped the matter. Though he knew it wouldn't be for long.

How many times could she be caught unawares with Julian in an improper position? First with Safina and then with his mother, of all people.

Cassie punched the pillow she was fluffing and tossed it onto the king-size bed with the flowing canopy overhead. This was by far one of the nicest suites she'd seen so far on the resort—"The Deluxe," it would be advertised as. Fit for a queen.

She could definitely see where Julian got his looks. The woman was stunning. And elegant. And classy.

All the things Cassie would never be. One had to be born with such an air about them. As much as she hated to admit it, Maria's arrival had made her confront all the ways she and Julian were so utterly different.

Not that it mattered. Maybe she'd lucked out back there. Maria's arrival had interrupted her near confession to Julian. Maybe that was for the best.

Why burden him with the knowledge? If she were smart, she would do her best to shine in this job, polish up her CV with it added, then get a glowing recommendation from Julian and move on with her life.

There was no need for Julian or his mother to know that she was pregnant by a man who wanted nothing to do with her. Cassie huffed out a breath and dropped down onto the bed then flung herself back onto the mattress.

How had her life become so complicated?

"I ask myself that almost daily," a masculine voice responded from the doorway.

Good heavens, she'd voiced the question out loud without even realizing. She should definitely get to that medical clinic. The hormones were completely disorienting her.

She bolted upright. "Julian. I was just finishing up."

He smiled at her with amusement shining in his eyes. "So I see."

"I mean, I did just finish up. Just testing the bed."

What an unoriginal thing to say. She cringed as soon as the words left her mouth.

Julian laughed and entered the room. "And how does it rate, then?"

"Um. Nice. It's really nice. I think she'll like it." She glanced around at the opulence surrounding her. Beige and black furnishings accented with the finest crafted fixtures. The entire wall opposite was clear glass, affording an unencumbered view of the sea in the distance. "I can't see how she'd be anything less than thrilled with the suite."

"One would hope," Julian said after releasing a deep sigh. "My mother can be a hard person to please at times."

"She's very lovely," It was the only word Cassie could think of that even came close to describing her. It took a lot to intimidate her; at least since she was a kid anyway. Maria Santigo definitely did the trick.

"I'll be sure to tell her you think so. She loves compliments."

Who didn't? Especially if they were well deserved.

"I guess I'll be going, then," she said, slowly stepping around him. "Let your mother get settled."

Julian reached for her before she took more than a few steps. Would the man's touch ever stop making her feel like jelly inside? Even under these circumstances she seemed to be defenseless. The feel of him against her skin should be the last thing on her mind.

"Was there something else?"

"Yes," Julian replied. "I want to show you something before you leave. It's a special feature in the deluxe suites. Revolutionary if I do say so myself."

Her curiosity was definitely piqued. What else could this amazing room boast in terms of comfort? In addition to a Jacuzzi tub and multiheaded marble shower and artwork that probably cost more than her whole apartment?

Julian led her to a wooden panel on the opposite wall. She'd assumed it was simply another clothing bureau. But when he opened the door, he revealed an elaborate board of some type with various knobs and switches. The words on the adjacent labels were in

Spanish. Cassie couldn't make out much except for one that she could have sworn meant flower.

"What is it?"

"A personal aromatherapy dispensing system," Julian replied.

"Aromatherapy? In the wall?"

Julian nodded. "State-of-the-art design." He reached over and turned one of the knobs. "Here. We'll try lavender."

In mere seconds a fine mist sprayed out of various corners of the room and the soothing scent of gentle lavender filled the air.

"It's like a speaker system, but for smell," Julian explained.

"Oh, my." Cassie was at a loss for words. She simply breathed deeply of the rich scent and let it soothe her frazzled nerves.

"Would you like to try?" Julian asked.

"Um…sure." She'd always liked the combination of lavender and vanilla scents together. It reminded her of the one trip to the Cape. The mother had a fancy glass bottle of lotion on the guest bathroom sink counter. Cassie had been too afraid to actually apply any, had simply indulged in a deep inhale every night before bed for the short time she'd been a guest there.

"Which one is vanilla?" she asked. Julian pointed to one of the switches. She flipped it up as he'd done with the lavender.

"And this knob controls the amount of scent dispensed," he added. She twisted it a quarter turn.

In no time, the delicious scent of vanilla intermingled with the lavender already floating through the air.

Cassie indulged in another deep breath.

"That's just heavenly, Julian. What a fantastic idea."

"I'm glad you like it." His smile was so genuine, so pure, she wanted to somehow capture it in a bottle. He was genuinely pleased that he'd impressed her.

Maybe it was the enticing scents floating in the air, maybe it was the luxurious setting of the opulent suite but something suddenly shifted in the air between them. Cassie knew she wasn't imaging it.

And she certainly wasn't imaging Julian leaning toward her. Before she knew it, he'd taken her chin between his fingers. Her breath caught in her throat as he drew closer. And then, before she could form another coherent thought, let alone speak, his lips were up against hers.

The merest brush, the gentlest kiss. But it was enough to send her heart soaring. He tasted of pure man and utter temptation. He tasted just as she'd imagined he would taste. God help her, she had imagined it. And the reality was so much better.

The sound of footsteps approaching the doorway served to pour a figurative fire over her skin.

She forced herself to pull away before whoever it was made their way into the room. She refused to be caught again. It had to be his mother.

Heart hammering, Cassie took a deep breath, willed her pulse to slow.

"Cassie—" Julian began, reaching for her once more.

But she held up a hand to stop him then silently walked out of the room, hoping Julian wouldn't follow her out.

She needed to be alone for a while to process what just happened. And to figure out exactly what she was going to do about it.

Because the fact of the matter was that she'd enjoyed it far too much.

CHAPTER NINE

THREE DAYS LATER, Cassie was in the shower when she felt a dreaded sensation in the pit of her stomach.

Something wasn't right. She could sense it down to her bones. She'd spent the night tossing and turning, attributing her restlessness to tiredness and anxiety. All night, she'd tried to tell herself that everything would be fine, that she just needed to slow down. But now, with an achy cramp developing right in the vicinity of her lower belly, she could no longer ignore what might very well be warning signs.

She squeezed her eyes shut and uttered a small prayer. *Please let my baby be okay.*

Gingerly stepping out of the porcelain tub, she toweled off as quickly as she could. There was nothing for it. She would have to apologize to Julian for the short notice but she desperately needed to take the day off and head into town to visit the medical clinic. She simply refused to risk the safety of her child.

Knowing Julian, he would insist on driving her. She didn't have it in her to turn him down. It would be the most expedient way to get there, after all. And maybe it was time to come clean to him about the pregnancy finally. The longer she kept it secret, the heavier it weighed on her.

First things first.

When she made it down to the lobby, he was already there, dressed in a cotton V-neck and pressed khaki pants. He looked like he'd been at work for several hours. Which was probably an accurate assessment. Specs of the activity grounds were spread on the counter before him. They were supposed to spend the morning going over further amenities to be added to the tennis courts. It would all have to wait.

Her sheer panic must have shown on her face. Julian dropped the pen he'd been holding and reached her in three long strides. "What's wrong, Cassie? Are you unwell again?"

Tears sprang in the backs of her eyes at

his concern. Tears of guilt and fear. A blatant urge to spill everything right then and there nearly overwhelmed her. But they simply didn't have the time right now. She would tell him after she met with the doctor.

"I'm afraid so," she answered him finally. "I plan on heading to the medical clinic. Just to be safe."

Julian didn't hesitate. As she'd anticipated, he ran behind the desk and lifted a set of car keys from one of the shelves. "Let's go."

"I can call a car service, Julian. You don't have to drop everything and—"

But he was ignoring her and gently nudging her toward the lobby doors. In no time, they were driving through the curvy, windy roads that led to the center of town. Julian insisted on escorting her inside once they got to the medical building.

Mere minutes after that, she was on an examining table waiting for the doctor.

The cramps were still plaguing her, though it hadn't gotten any worse, thank God. She continued her silent prayers while she waited.

Finally, after what seemed like an eternity

but was possibly a few minutes, a physician appeared and greeted her in accented English.

He was a short, balding man with kind eyes, and Cassie imagined he'd be the lovable uncle if she'd had any kind of family to call her own.

After a thorough physical examination, he gave her a gentle smile of reassurance. "I think you can relax. Everything seems in order."

Cassie couldn't help the tears of relief that started rolling down her cheeks. "It's fairly common to have some slight cramping during the first trimester."

She wanted to hug him and give him a sloppy kiss on the cheek all at once.

He continued, "To be on the safe side, however, I'd like to keep you for a few hours. Preferably overnight if that's all right with you."

Cassie nodded, endlessly grateful for the man's thoroughness.

"We'll continually monitor the baby via cardiogram. Just to put all minds at ease. I'm sure your husband would agree."

Cassie nodded immediately, agreeing to the

recommendation. She didn't bother to correct him about the husband. What was the point? It would only lead to speculation and questions she didn't want to have to deal with just yet.

"A nurse will take you to an overnight room upstairs," the doctor told her. "Sit here for a few minutes."

Once he left, Cassie took a moment to breathe and try to get her thoughts in order. All that mattered was that her baby was safe and sound. But now she had to face the emotional toll of confessing to a man, whom she'd come to care for deeply, all that she'd been keeping from him.

Now that her panic had subsided somewhat, another type of fear had started to creep in. It curled like a predatory serpent in the hollow of her chest and squeezed tight. She would have to explain to Julian exactly what was going on. There could be no delaying it at this point. It wasn't fair to deny him the knowledge any longer. Her courage had failed her long enough and she had to summon it somehow. He had a right to know. Not only as her boss, but because of all that he had grown to mean to her when she hadn't been paying attention.

How would she find the words?

A knock sounded on the door. It had to be the nurse arriving to lead her upstairs. Cassie would be sure to ask the woman to send Julian up as soon as she was settled.

"Come in."

But she was mistaken. The person who stepped into the room wasn't any nurse. It was Julian himself. And it was obvious from the blatant look of shock on his face that she wouldn't have to confess to him, after all.

He already knew.

Tonto!

How many times in one lifetime could he behave so foolishly? And over a woman. Again.

Everything made so much sense now in hindsight. But he'd been too blind to see what was in front of his face all this time.

Cassie was pregnant. No doubt it was Carlos's baby. But he couldn't know that for certain. Though it was a possibility that made complete sense. And she hadn't seen fit to tell him. Not even after what had been developing between them.

Was she still in love with Carlos? How deeply? Even now, the thought sent a bolt of fury through him. That made him beyond ridiculous. History repeating itself. Because apparently, he would never learn. He hadn't even begun to face what he was feeling for her. Now he was stunned and reeling from the revelation that had hit him like a fleet of trucks several moments ago.

It had taken nearly ten minutes of pacing the hallway before he'd worked up the ability to walk into her room. More than one nurse cast curious glances his way, clearly wondering why he hadn't yet gone in to check on the mother of his child.

If they only knew. Hell, if he'd only known.

How could he not have seen it coming? The way Carlos had insisted his envelope be hand-delivered in a package to a woman in Boston. His untrustworthy "cousin" had made it seem like barely more than a business transaction. But he should have seen through it. Yet another time he'd given Carlos Alhambra the benefit of the doubt only to have his naivete thrown back in his face.

No matter what happened, Cassie would always be tied with Carlos in the most monumental of ways. The two would have a permanent connection for the rest of their lives, regardless of how she felt about him. He knew he was being a selfish bastard but the idea had bile churning in his gut and burning through to his core.

Carlos didn't deserve a woman like Cassie.

I want Cassie all to myself.

She still sat perched on the examining table, a look of question and turmoil written all over her face.

"The staff assumed I was your husband or boyfriend," he explained what she was silently asking him to confirm.

Cassie opened her mouth to speak but no words left her lips. The color had completely drained from her skin. She was even paler now than when she'd rushed downstairs earlier back at the resort in a panic. Suddenly, an overwhelming feeling of guilt washed over him. She was here after what had to be a harrowing scare. And all he could think about was what he'd just discovered and the implications for *him*.

He had to calm down, look at the bigger picture. They would talk soon enough. He would get a chance to ask her all the questions scrambling through his brain. But this was neither the place nor the time.

Cassie made another attempt to speak. "Julian, you have to under—"

He held up a hand to stop her. "Later, *bella*. I just came to check on you."

"You—you did?"

He could only nod. "I understand they're taking you upstairs to spend the night. What do you need to make your stay more comfortable?"

Tears began to pool in her eyes before slowly rolling down her cheeks. *Dios!* He couldn't stand to see a woman cry. Especially not this woman. Now he felt like an even bigger heel. Though he knew he could hardly be blamed for his reaction out in the waiting area—he'd just received the shock of his life out there, after all. Still, the thought of her weeping due in part to him in any way made him want to rush over and take her in his arms. He forced himself to resist the temptation. He stepped back toward the door instead.

Cassie dropped her chin down to her chest and swiped the tears away with the palms of her hands. "Um, thank you. That's very kind. I have a toiletry bag near the shower stall in my suite."

"Got it."

"And there's a set of pajamas folded up on the bed." She looked up again, flashed him a small, false smile. "They're definitely more comfortable than this," she added, lifting the wide, gaping collar of her hospital gown.

He couldn't find it within himself to return her smile, not even with a fake one of his own. "I'll be sure you get them. Anything else?"

She shook her head. "I don't think so."

"Send me a text if you think of anything else after I leave."

"Thank you, Julian. Really."

"You're welcome."

"And…"

"Yes?" he asked, though he could guess what was next to come.

"I'm sorry."

It was Julian's turn to look away. "Me too, Cassie." He meant it. He was so sorry that he couldn't be more for her right then. He couldn't be what she needed. Didn't have it in him.

She hadn't trusted him enough to tell him until the truth came out on its own completely by accident. She hadn't wanted him to know.

Was it some type of loyalty to Carlos that had driven her decision? Again, bile rose up in his throat that she might be trying to protect or shield the other man because she cared for him.

What did that mean for him? Had she felt any of the emotions that he'd been developing toward her?

Most likely not.

He turned around and left to go retrieve her things from back at the resort. Unable to watch her tears any longer.

And unwilling to trust himself not to go to her even now.

She should have corrected the doctor as soon as he'd voiced his flawed assumption.

It hadn't even occurred to her that he would go find Julian and inadvertently cause this current catastrophe. Cassie watched the door shut behind him now and blinked back oncoming tears.

The look of derision on Julian's face when he'd first walked in would stay with her for the rest of her life. She would see it every time she closed her eyes. He had every right to look at her that way. How would she ever be able to explain the exact reasons why she hadn't come clean much earlier?

He'd told her they would talk later. Cassie had no clue what she would say. The only real option was to answer his questions as best and as honestly as she could. And then she'd just have to wait for the fallout and accept whatever it might be.

For all she knew, she might not even have a job any longer.

No. She refused to believe Julian could be so callous. He was no Martin Gregor, her manager back in Boston.

Julian cared for her. And she'd misled him. She might have never lied to him outright, but was a lie of omission any better? All she needed was a chance to try and explain. There had never been a good time to tell Julian. At first he'd been nothing more than a temporary boss. Not the man she'd been falling in love with.

And she had to acknowledge the reality for what it was. She was indeed falling in love with Julian Santigo.

Cassie sucked in a deep breath and grabbed a tissue from the nearby counter. She'd find a way to talk to him, though it was hard to figure out exactly what to say. She would just have to cross that bridge when she came to it.

The healthiest thing to do right now was to focus fully on this baby and the life she wanted to ensure for him or her. All she wanted was for this child to be happy and healthy and guaranteed a secure future, unlike what she'd been dealt in life herself.

Julian was hurt as a direct result of her actions.

He'd actually physically recoiled from her at one point. She'd thought her heart would shatter into a million pieces at that very moment. Something akin to physical pain had struck her at the disappointment so clear in his eyes. His kindness about bringing back her things from her suite only added salt to the wound. How could he still be so nice to her even now?

By the time they took her upstairs and set her up in a room, she was utterly exhausted. Between the terrifying scare she'd given herself about the baby and the emotional toll of Julian's reaction, Cassie wanted nothing more than to close her eyes and sink into the oblivion of sleep. So she didn't even resist the urge.

When she woke up later, she had no idea how long she'd been out. A slew of cords and cables were attached to her stomach area and led to a monitor above her bed. With a startle, she realized she was no longer alone. Her toiletries bag and some articles of clothing, including her pajamas, sat on the tray cart next to her bed.

Julian.

But as her eyes regained focus, she realized it wasn't him who sat by her bedside, staring at a tablet. Rather, it was a different Santigo. For some reason, Julian's mother was in her room. Cassie blinked to make sure she wasn't seeing things or in some kind of dreamlike state after her nap.

"You're awake," the older woman greeted her with a smile.

"Uh...yes."

"Feeling better?"

What she was feeling was confusion. "Yes, thank you." It was so hard to resist asking her outright what she was doing there. Then it occurred to her. Julian had promised to bring her things back, but he had no desire to do so himself. He didn't want to be anywhere near her.

Maria's words confirmed her conclusion. "Julian asked me to come check up on you."

"I see."

Maria reached over and patted her hand. "He's very concerned about you. But was called away on a maintenance issue."

Right. A maintenance issue. Sure he was. Cassie didn't believe that for a moment.

"You didn't need to take time out of your day to sit here with me, Senora Santigo," Cassie told her, though part of her couldn't help but feel touched that the woman had. She was barely more than a stranger to Julian's mother yet she'd spent a good amount of time sitting by her bedside.

"You must call me Maria, remember?"

She didn't deserve the kindness of these people. And how much did Maria know? Had Julian told her exactly what her situation was? Did she know Cassie carried the child she might consider her niece or nephew? Dear heavens! What if she thought the baby was Julian's?

The horrified expression on her face and her audible gasp must have conveyed her questions wordlessly. Maria squeezed the hand she'd been patting.

"You don't have to explain anything to me, dear."

Okay. It appeared Julian hadn't told her much if anything, then.

"I don't?"

Maria shook her head with a sympathetic smile. "No. Julian asked me to bring your things and make sure you were doing all right. I wanted to stay for a while because I thought you might want the company. I wouldn't want to wake up alone in a strange room in a foreign country with a slew of tubes stuck to my stomach myself."

Cassie wasn't sure what to say. How could she express the wealth of gratitude she felt right now? Maria was completely right. Cassie's first reaction upon awakening would have been disoriented anxiety. Being alone would have added to that anxiety. She'd been alone so often in her past during major life moments. She really was glad for the company. It didn't matter one bit that she didn't know Julian's mother that well. All that mattered was that the other woman seemed kind and concerned about her. She could count on one hand all the people that might fall into that category.

A day ago, she might have included Julian in that number. Funny how much of a difference one day could make.

"Thank you, Maria. Really. I can't tell you how much I appreciate it."

The other woman's eyes shone with kindness and understanding. "You're welcome. You're not the first woman to find herself in this predicament. You won't be the last."

There was so much Cassie could read into

that statement. But one thing was crystal clear. Maria didn't think Cassie was carrying her grandchild. Her mind betrayed her by imagining that very thing. In a more perfect universe, the baby would belong to someone as decent and caring as Julian. The kind woman who'd just sat with her for however long was everything she could have wanted in a mother-in-law or grandparent for her baby.

No! She had to completely shut out that thinking.

Reality was what it was. And she would just have to accept it. All of it.

Maria Santigo was still sitting at her bedside when she awoke again two hours later. Cassie knew she should be glad for it, that the other woman hadn't left her in all this time. But she couldn't help the nudge of disappointment in her center that the person sitting in the room with her wasn't Julian.

How selfish of her.

Her sleep had been fitful and restless. Dreams of Julian walking away from her as she tried to talk to him had taken several variations through her imagination. It didn't help that she was hooked up to a monitor via uncomfortable cords and wires. It was impossible to move and change her position.

Overall, Cassie felt miserable and sorry for herself. She also felt guilty for being anything less than grateful that her baby was okay.

Maria gave her a gentle smile and looked up from some type of knitting project she held in her hands when she realized Cassie was awake.

"Can I get you anything, dear?"

"No, thank you. Though I feel bad that you've been stuck here all this time."

Maria waved a dismissive hand at those words. "Don't worry about that. Julian stopped by earlier and dropped off some knitting I'd been looking forward to finishing."

Cassie sat up straighter against her pillow despite herself. "He was here?" She wanted to kick something in frustration—she'd missed him. It would have been a soothing balm to her soul to be able to see him if only for a few minutes. To be able to look into his eyes and try to gauge exactly how disappointed in her he was.

But maybe it was just as well. The awkwardness between them would no doubt be practically tangible.

Maria nodded in answer to her question. "He didn't want to wake you."

She had to ask her next question. "Um… how is he?"

Maria quirked an eyebrow. "He's, how do you Americans say it…? *Processing*, I believe is the right term."

Cassie rubbed her palm down her face. That was as good an answer as she could hope to get.

Maria suddenly released a deep sigh and set her knitting down on the windowsill. She fixed a steady gaze on Cassie's face.

"How much has my son told you, *mija*?"

The unexpected question threw Cassie off for a moment. She was more focused on all that she hadn't told *him*.

"About what?"

"About himself. Anything?"

Thinking about the answer gave Cassie pause. All she really knew about Julian was that he was a successful businessman who'd stepped up to take care of his family after they'd lost their beloved patriarch.

Upon examination, she realized she knew very little about the man she'd come to care so much for in such a short period of time.

Maria released another sigh. Sitting in front of the window, with the sunlight bathing her in light from behind she looked almost ethereal. Her dark hair hung in wavy curls down to her shoulders. She looked more like she could be one of Cassie's girlfriends, hardly old enough to be Julian's mother.

"I thought so," she began. "I won't betray his confidence by getting into details. That's up to him to share with you. And I do hope he will."

Cassie hoped so too. But she didn't think the prospect of Julian sharing much about himself was very likely. If he hadn't done so already.

"My son hasn't opened his heart up to too many people in his life. The last time he did, he had it broken."

Cassie had to swallow past the lump that had formed in her throat. Julian had cared for someone. Someone who'd hurt him. A twinge of something she didn't want to examine pierced the area around her heart. She refused to acknowledge it as jealousy.

"I see," she managed to utter.

"It wasn't so much that the relationship didn't work out."

"It wasn't?"

Maria shook her head. "Truth be told, I didn't have high expectations that the relationship would stand the test of time. They were two very different people with very different lives."

The same could easily be said about her and Julian, as well. Cassie didn't voice the thought out loud.

Maria continued. "No. It was more that he was caught completely unawares when it happened. He didn't see it coming at all. He felt humiliated about the way things ended. Totally unprepared."

Maria's message was coming through loud and clear.

"Julian felt his trust was betrayed," Cassie supplied the obvious.

"That's right. On top of the disappointment of a failed relationship, there was the knowledge that she'd kept it all from him. He thought he had his future all set out in front of him. No less than what he deserved after we lost my beloved Rafael and all that Julian had accomplished since his father's death." Maria reached over and gently patted her hand. "He pulled away after that. From everyone. You should be prepared for that."

Cassie nodded, understanding exactly what Maria was trying to tell her. There was only one question that remained—was it already too late?

CHAPTER TEN

SHE WALKED THE property for close to forty minutes before she found him. But she was determined. It was time they hashed some things out. She would pay heed to everything Maria had confided in her back at the hospital last evening.

He was conferring with the plumbing contractor by the smaller infinity pool at the edge of the property.

Julian subtly dismissed the other man when he saw Cassie approach. Clearly her determination was written on her face judging by the resigned look in his eyes.

"Something I can do for you, Cassie?"

So formal, so distant. As if he hadn't gently and tenderly kissed her just a few short days ago in the deluxe suite amidst the tempting aroma of lavender and vanilla.

"In fact, there is. We need to talk, don't you think?"

He shrugged lightly. "Do we?"

Cassie's jaw dropped. How could he be so cavalier at this moment? "I'd say so."

He motioned to the chair opposite him. But she was too agitated to sit. Instead she stepped even closer to him, hands placed on her hips.

"I'm sorry, Julian. I figured I'd say it again."

He looked away out toward the beach. In the distance the Mediterranean shone like jewelry under the bright Spanish sun. Any other time, Cassie would have liked to simply stare at the scene, enjoy the sheer beauty of it.

"All right," was all Julian said.

"That's it? That's all you have to say?"

He squinted up at her, not bothering to block the sun from his eyes. "What precisely are you apologizing for?"

Wasn't it obvious? "For not telling you sooner. I can only say that I meant to. Countless times." She refused to apologize for being pregnant. Regardless of the circumstances or the unfortunate connection to Julian. As far as she was concerned, this baby was a gift. She would never see her child as anything but.

He inhaled sharply. "I see. Then thank you. I accept your apology."

Cassie wanted to reach over and take him by the shoulders, make him look at her squarely. "Julian, please. Just say something. More than empty words that hold no truth."

He was silent for so long that Cassie almost gave up and began to turn to walk away. "All right, then. I guess I could ask you a question."

Finally, maybe they were getting somewhere. "Anything. Please, ask me anything. I promise to be as honest as possible."

He actually smirked at her statement. Cassie decided to let that go, simply waited for him to begin.

"When exactly had you considered telling me? Was it that day on the boat when you first felt ill? That seemed like an opportune time. Or perhaps even earlier, maybe after I picked you up at the airport. Then there was the time in the deluxe suite. We were all alone then. I somehow missed all these attempts you must have made that somehow led to your secret remaining just that."

He didn't understand how vulnerable she

felt those specific times he mentioned. They were barely more than strangers during that drive from the airport. She wasn't anywhere near ready or willing to divulge personal information to a man she'd just recently met. And the day on the boat had been her first ever real experience with morning sickness. It had taken all she had to just get on solid land and regain her equilibrium. Then his mother had shown up unexpectedly, throwing her yet another curveball.

There was no sense in explaining any of that. Julian wasn't willing to hear the actual words. "I can only tell you that every time I worked up the nerve, circumstances seemed to impede my resolve. I never meant to be dishonest, Julian. I intended to my job to the best of my ability for the time I'd been contracted for. Without complications."

"All right, then. There is nothing more to say regarding the matter." He made a move to stand but she reached out and stopped him with a hand on his shoulder.

"Would you mind indulging me in a question or two, as well?" she asked after several beats.

He nodded once, not even looking at her. "By all means."

"Are you considering terminating me?"

His jaw dropped at the question. To his credit, he seemed genuinely surprised, as if the thought hadn't even crossed his mind.

"Of course you're not being terminated. All that matters to me is that you can do the job and do it without jeopardizing your health or that of—" He stopped midsentence, as if he couldn't even bring himself to say the word.

"I had to ask, had to know for sure."

"You can be certain. In fact, we're due to tour a nearby site of ruins to evaluate its potential as an excursion option. Ruines Romanes de Pollentia. If you're up for it, that is."

She gave him a quick nod. "Yes. I'm up for it."

"You won't be taxing yourself?" he asked, genuine concern in his tone.

"I won't. The doctor gave me the go-ahead to resume all regular activities."

"Touring ruins is hardly regular."

Cassie tried not to snap. "I'll be fine, Julian."

"Great. It's settled." He tried to step away

but she stopped him. "Wait. One more question," she began.

Julian pinched the bridge of his nose. She had the sense he was barely holding on to his patience and composure. She'd heard about the fiery nature of Spanish men. If it were true, he'd done a good job of keeping that side of him in check. She didn't think it would be prudent to try and goad it out of him, however.

After all, at least she still had a job she'd like to keep. And he was still her boss.

"Go ahead," Julian said, continuing to look away from her.

"Why did you send your mother yesterday to come sit with me? You could have just dropped off my things. Heck, you could have even had them delivered via one of the crew. Yet you sent your mother. Why?"

Julian finally looked at her, crossed his arms in front of his chest. "It's no great mystery. Safina had the day off. And I figured you'd prefer the company of a woman. Another mother, at that. It seemed the most logical thing to do."

Cassie worked hard not to betray the feeling of relief that infused through her at those seemingly innocuous words. Even at his most stunned state, he had cared enough to consider what was best for her then acted on it.

"You were right on all counts," she said, by way of thanking him. "Your mother was a tremendous source of comfort while I was laid up."

He shrugged. "Glad to hear it."

His answer had told her more than he could imagine. And more than she could have hoped for.

Maybe she wasn't too late, after all.

Julian knew he wasn't going to be able to avoid her for long. He'd almost felt a sense of relief when he'd noticed her charging toward him during his meeting with the master plumber.

Not that he'd had any idea what he was going to say to her.

The truth was, he'd missed her. As much as he hated to admit it to himself. He was beginning to forget what this place was like before her arrival. Even knowing what he knew now about the pregnancy, he dreaded the day that she'd leave for good.

That was why his heart had lurched when she asked about the job. For a second, he'd been afraid she was ready to quit and walk away.

Heaven help him. He was in deep. With a woman who was expecting another man's baby. His own adopted *cousin's* baby, at that.

Every time he thought about the child's parentage, he wanted to throw something against the wall. Carlos was reckless, immature and irresponsible. Here he was, blessed with this gift that he'd evidently turned his back on. Some men didn't realize how lucky they had it. Not the first time he'd pondered that quandary about life.

He was expecting Cassie to turn and walk away now that they'd finally addressed the issue at hand. But to his surprise, she finally pulled the chair out in front of him and plopped herself down to sit at the table with him.

"I promise you, if I thought for one moment when I accepted this opportunity that my condition would impede my abilities, I would have turned you down flat."

He could only nod.

"Do you trust me enough to believe that's true?" she asked.

"Trust is a two-way street, Cassie."

She quirked an eyebrow. Then shifted in her seat, leaning forward with her elbows on the table. He had her full interest.

"Let's face facts, shall we?" he began. "The truth is that at no point did you trust me enough to tell me what was happening."

She flinched as if struck and he felt a piercing stab of guilt. But he didn't regret saying the words. She was asking for full disclosure, and she would get it. Even if she hadn't afforded him the same courtesy.

"You mentioned earlier that you hated being made a fool of. And being taken for granted."

"What of it?"

"What happened? I know I have no right to ask, but I'm asking anyway."

Julian had to chuckle. If only she'd been exposed to Spanish tabloids and websites two years ago. She would know the whole story.

"You don't keep up much with the royal

families of the world, I take it?" he asked, surprised he was willing to go down this road with her. He'd spent the last two years refusing to so much as speak of the matter even with members of his own family.

"I'm afraid not. Not even up to speed on the goings-on of the British monarchy."

Julian had figured as much. "I was engaged a couple years ago," he said, simply blurting it out.

She visibly reacted, subtly yet physically startling where she sat. "Engaged? I don't understand."

He raised an eyebrow at her.

"I mean, I understand the being engaged part." Though clearly it had taken her by surprise. "But what does that have to do with any kind of royal family?"

Julian rested his arms on the glass table between them, as well. "My former fiancée is Princess Rosa Marisa de la Garza."

Cassie's jaw fell open. "You were about to marry a princess?"

"*Sí.*"

"And you two broke up?" she asked, she

seemed to have trouble summoning the words, tripped over them.

"Not exactly. *We* didn't break up. She broke up with me. Left me at the altar, as a matter of fact."

"Oh, Julian."

"Her betrothal to a titled Spanish baron had been arranged since birth. But she assured me she wanted nothing to do with an arranged marriage. That she wanted to marry for love. Even if it meant disownment from her family and estrangement from all her loved ones. I believed her. I never should have."

He wouldn't go into the rest of it, he decided. There was no need to tell her about the mansion he'd purchased for Rosa along the Spanish countryside, the renovations they'd planned in anticipation of a large family as she'd spoken countless times of her desire to have at least three children. All the plans they'd made that she'd found so easy to turn her back on in the end.

"Ultimately, she chose the titles and lifestyle over me. I found out the hard way she was simply living some last-minute family rebellion fantasy which she took much too far.

She's married to the baron now. They have a toddler son, who just turned one, I believe."

Cassie remained silent for a long time. He'd truly shocked her. Actually, he'd shocked himself somewhat. After months of refusing to even discuss his doomed nuptials, he was surprised by how easily sharing it all with her had come. Also surprising was the lack disappointment that usually pummeled his midsection at the mention of Rosa's name. Not a development he'd seen coming.

"I propose we start anew," she told him after several more moments of complete silence, finally returning to the present. "We agree that there will be no more secrets. Decide that we're going to trust each other." She held out her hand. "Deal?"

Julian released a deep breath then reached out and took her hand in his. "Deal."

A princess. He'd been engaged to a real-life, honest-to-goodness, royal bloodline Spanish princess. Cassie felt a bubble of laughter swell up in her chest and threaten to escape her throat as she left the pool area to make her way back to her room.

To think, she'd been fighting an attraction to him, had speculated that he might find her attractive in return, despite the circumstances. How utterly ridiculous of her.

When she reached her suite, she succumbed to her curiosity and pulled out her laptop then called up her browser's search engine. A simple query on Julian's name brought window after window of images and write-ups chronicling the whirlwind romance followed by the ill-fated wedding that never happened.

Julian's princess was stunning. Dark hair, gorgeous figure, aristocratic face. Even pictures of her while pregnant looked elegant. Not a hint of frump anywhere in sight. Everything one would expect of a European noble. She had a look about her that bespoke of the class and breeding she'd been born into.

Things Cassie could never hope to achieve no matter how hard she tried.

CHAPTER ELEVEN

SHE'D NEVER SEEN anything like it. Likely would never see anything quite comparable again. Cassie felt completely at a loss for words as she studied the ancient ruins of what was long ago a Roman city. She had her work cut out for her if she was going to come up with the words to try and describe this place for any kind of marketing write-up.

"This is amazing, Julian," she told him, not for the first time since they'd arrived. The Ruines Romanes de Pollentia consisted of three different areas of what was once an ancient Roman town—a residential area, the theater and the forum. The latter would have been the center of the old city which housed the temples, commercial buildings and administration structures.

"It's almost beyond contemplation that we're looking at the remnants of a town that existed centuries ago."

"I've always found it quite impressive."

They currently stood at the residential portion of the ruins, known as La Portella. Cassie had done a good amount of reading about the archaeological site as soon as Julian had told her about their planned trip the other day.

"It's beyond impressive," she commented now. "There are three separate houses in La Portella. All of them designed around an atrium to let in air and light."

Julian chuckled softly next to her. "You've been doing your research, I see."

She nodded. "I intend to mark this as a highlight of the excursion options. Say it's highly recommended. Such history." She paused suddenly. The decision wasn't solely hers. "That is, if you agree."

"I'll let you take the lead with this one, Cassie. You seem to know where you want to go with it."

She did indeed. Had all sorts of ideas. Now that Julian knew about the baby and the pregnancy scare was behind her, Cassie felt as if a weight had been lifted.

She just had to stop thinking about the fact

that the man standing next to her had almost become a prince by marriage.

Stop it.

Here and now, it behooved her to focus on the professional reason she was here.

"I just don't understand how you could have had any doubt that we should include this place as part of our itinerary offerings."

Julian shrugged. "I needed your feedback. Many tourists are happy to simply tan all day and go swimming. Mallorca has a beautiful coastline with several pristine beaches to offer."

She thought about that. "Speaking as a Boston native, I think a good number of American tourists would want to experience the history of the island. This is an ideal place to learn about at least part of it."

Julian gave her a mini salute. "Then it's official. The ruins will be a destination spot on one of our packages. Let's head over to the theater, shall we?"

It took about fifteen minutes to leisurely walk from the residential part down to where the remains of an ancient arena now stood. A raised semicircle of stone that must have once been seating faced a center stage area. Cassie knew from her reading that the theater had been used for everything from sporting events to plays and musical performances. The ancient Romans who'd conquered this part of the island weren't all that different from today's entertainment fans.

Together, she and Julian walked past the seating area toward the stage. A sudden movement by her feet had her startled enough that she jumped and nearly toppled over. Julian reached out to grab her right before she fell.

"Dios," he said softly, still holding on to her tightly. "Careful. You don't need to be falling in your condition."

"I'd say falling in any condition would be less than ideal," she responded, with a flippancy she didn't feel. Being in Julian's arms again had her heart stirring in her chest. All too soon, he set her straight back on her feet and released her from his grip.

"What was that?"

"I'm guessing it was a lizard. Or some other critter who likes to hang around archaeological sites."

Cassie shuddered. She hadn't come across too many lizards during her New England upbringing.

"They're not terribly common in this part of the island but they aren't unheard of," Julian added as she tried to resume her normal breathing.

She looked up to find a family of three staring at her with concern. The mother gestured in their direction. *"Estás bien?"*

"Sí," Julian answered, then added that she'd simply been startled.

Cassie gave the family a reassuring smile and they continued exploring the site. A pang of longing settled around her chest as she watched them. A mother, a father and a young girl of about six or seven years of age. The parents held hands as their daughter twirled around the stage area, clearly pretending she was putting on a show. Both mom and dad gave her indulgent smiles and applause.

Cassie had to look away from the touching scene, as charming as it was. She had to face the reality that she might never have that. All her life, she'd sworn to herself that when she became a parent, she would try to do everything right. She would try to be as different from her own mother as was humanly possible. She planned to fully adhere to that vow to the best of her ability. But alas, the idyllic family life that she'd imagined for herself was not meant to be. Cassie had to accept that and move on.

Abruptly, she turned on her heel to walk higher up the stone seats, away from Julian, feigning a deep interest in the upper part of the theater.

The truth was that she didn't want him to notice the tears threatening to fall from her stinging eyes.

While Cassie had been watching the family of tourists, Julian had been watching her.

The ache of longing on her face was as clear as the bright blue sky above them. For the umpteenth time since finding out the truth, Julian cursed his cousin for the carelessness with which he'd treated Cassie.

She deserved so much more. She was smart, dedicated, talented. He'd meant it when he'd told her that she was going to make a fabulous mom. Cassie Wells was one of those people who embraced life fully and gave all of themselves. Despite the hardships she'd dealt with growing up, she'd achieved professional success and had done it completely on her own.

He watched her now as she climbed up to the highest level of the theater steps. With a weariness in her shoulders that he could see from where he stood far below, she slowly seated herself on one of the stones.

Julian rubbed a hand down his face. He knew he wasn't responsible for Carlos's misdeeds. But that didn't mean he didn't wish with all his soul that he could do something to make this whole situation with Cassie right.

Her whole demeanor had changed since they'd first arrived. Gone was the exuberance and excitement when she'd first laid eyes on this place. He debated going to her versus giving her some time to herself. The argument was short-lived. He wanted to be by her side.

He walked up the steps and sat down next to her.

"I just wanted to see the view from up here," she told him. Without conscious thought, he'd sat down close enough that their knees touched. He could smell the flowery scent of her shampoo. The warmth of her skin through her cotton sundress permeated his own.

"We don't have to talk about it if you like. But I'm here if you do."

She laughed softly. "Am I that easy to read, then?"

"I'm sorry, Cassie. I can leave you alone if you wish."

Her reply was immediate. "No. Please don't."

He didn't move. For several moments, they both sat in silence. Finally, Cassie spoke. "You know, there are so many horror stories out there about the American foster care system. I didn't find that to be the case."

"Oh?"

She shook her head. "I guess I was one of the lucky ones. Most of the families I was assigned to took their responsibility as foster homes seriously and tried to do right by it."

"I'm glad to hear it." He didn't say any more, just waited for her to finish.

"So I knew quite well what is was like to belong to a good, stable home with reliable parents who asked about grades and tried hard to make me feel welcome."

He remembered what she'd said about her mother showing up again and again to try and reclaim her. He couldn't imagine how disruptive that must have been to a child or young teen.

He didn't know how to answer her so he simply took her hand in his. She didn't try to pull it away.

"Can we sit here awhile longer?" she asked after several moments of silence. "I'm going to try and distract myself by imagining what kind of plays they may have staged here all those centuries ago."

He gave her hand a slight squeeze before responding. "We can stay as long as you like."

She turned to him then, her radiant smile back in place. It shocked him how much seeing that smile on her face sent a surge of pleasure clear to his toes, knowing that in a small way he'd helped bring that smile back after the sadness she'd just displayed.

Heaven help him, he wanted to be the man who gave her a reason to smile.

* * *

A week had passed since the day she and Julian had visited the ruins. A week in which the entire world seemed to have changed. She was actually beginning to show. Not much, but the small baby bump was there if one bothered to look carefully enough. She couldn't seem to stop caressing and palming that area of her stomach. Several times now, she'd looked up to find Julian catching her in the act of doing just that.

More than once, she'd found herself wishing that she could share the novel experience with someone. That she could share it with him specifically. And that was just downright silly on her part. Especially now that she'd found out about his past as a near member of the Spanish royal family.

Walking down past the front counter and toward the office area, she was surprised to find he wasn't alone at his desk. There was a woman in there with him. He appeared to be having her sign a document.

Something about her looked oddly familiar. Cassie was in the process of squinting through his open door to get a better look when Julian noticed her presence.

He motioned for her to come inside. "Cassie, glad you're here. I'd like you to meet our latest hire."

He'd hired someone without her input? Or even her knowledge?

Something was amiss. What was she missing? Had she overlooked a memo or email he'd sent?

Then she placed the woman—one of the nurses from her stay at the clinic a week ago. One of the agenda items on their massive to-do list was to hire a medical professional for the resort to be available on-site for emergencies. But it was nowhere near a top priority item. In fact, there was no need to bring one on board for the role weeks before any guests were even expected.

"You remember Larrisa, I hope," Julian was saying.

"Of course." Cassie reached out her hand. "Nice to see you again, Larrisa. Thanks for taking such great care of me a few days ago."

She looked at Julian in question. He answered her unspoken query. "I've decided to get the medical office staffed just to get it out of the way."

"I see."

The nurse flashed a smile in her direction. "I understand I'll be practicing until the guests arrive."

"Practicing?"

The other woman nodded. "You can help keep me sharp until the resort clientele arrives."

Cassie was slowly starting to put together what might have been happening. She didn't know whether to chastise Julian or give him a tight hug and sloppy kiss. "How would I do that?"

"Well, you're not too far along. So, I'd say weekly blood pressure checks and a quick listen with the stethoscope to start. And we'll just be sure you're getting adequate nutrition and staying hydrated."

"I see."

"We can start this week if that's all right with you."

"Of course."

After they'd said their goodbyes, Cassie watched as Larrisa walked out then paced to the door and shut it behind her. "You hired a nurse."

He nodded. "I did. It had to be done eventually."

"Yes, but it didn't have to be done this quickly."

"No reason to put it off."

"Thank you, Julian."

He didn't try to hide his motives. He'd hired her a private nurse because he'd learned she was pregnant. And she wasn't going to pretend she didn't appreciate it. She told him as much. "All I want is what's best for this baby. And I'm not too proud to turn this down. I appreciate you helping to ensure we're both being taken care of." *Unlike the actual father*, she added silently.

She turned to flee before she could say or do anything out of gratitude that she was sure to regret later. But she stopped suddenly at the sound of his voice before she could leave.

"Cassie," he said behind her as she reached for the doorknob.

"Yes?"

"When the time comes, you're going to make a fabulous mom."

CHAPTER TWELVE

THE NEXT MORNING, Cassie stood in the middle of a beautiful botanical garden. Only the plants around her weren't what one would expect in this part of the world. She was surrounded by cacti.

This was to be another one of the excursions offered through the resort, and she and Julian were here for firsthand exposure.

"Who would have ever thought that there would be a place specifically to see cactus plants on a Spanish island in the Mediterranean?" she said to Julian as they wandered around the large sprigs, some of them several meters long.

"Some of these are centuries old," Julian told her. "They're protected by these artificial terraces to encourage their growth."

From there they moved on to walk along the man-made lake surrounded by bamboo trees.

"This is nothing like the Boston Common,"

Cassie commented. "That's the closest thing to a botanical garden that I've been to."

"So it will do as a resort excursion, then?" he asked her.

"I'd absolutely say so." Julian's responding smile was strained and forced. In fact, he'd seemed distant and distracted all morning.

Cassie hoped deep in her heart that his demeanor had nothing to do with her. They'd reached an agreement, hadn't they? A truce of sorts. She didn't want to spoil the trip by bringing it up. Maybe she'd ask back at the hotel. But every instinct she possessed told her she wasn't imagining things. Something was on Julian's mind.

An hour later they were eating lunch at a charming tapas-style café by the sea. Cassie sipped orange juice while Julian enjoyed a tall glass of red sangria. The fruity aroma of his drink was almost as good as being able to taste it.

Though still concerned about what had Julian so distracted, Cassie allowed herself to indulge in the delicious food and fresh squeezed juice. Fresh fish, tangy olives and crispy bread served as a lunch fit for a princess.

She cringed internally at her choice of words. Thank goodness she hadn't said them out loud. She would have been mortified.

Once the plates were cleared, Julian made no move to get up. That was fine with her. She wanted to prolong this pleasant afternoon as long as possible. They'd be back to the reality of resort business soon enough.

But Julian's next sentence brought business reality to the forefront. It also shed light on the mystery of what must have been bothering him all morning.

"There's something we should discuss, Cassie."

Uh-oh. That sounded like it was bad news. She physically braced herself by leaning over the table.

"I'm afraid I received some news this morning that might jeopardize the success of the Paraiso's opening," he informed her before handing her his phone. The screen displayed some type of article from a Spanish leisure magazine.

"What does it say?"

"It's a write-up about the resort. I'm afraid my reputation has not been to my advantage."

She gave her head a brisk shake, wishing she knew enough Spanish to comprehend what the article said. "I don't understand."

"The author is questioning why a single bachelor would open an exclusive resort aimed specifically for women. She writes that it would make more sense for the proprietors to be female in order to understand their clientele better. She's reserving judgment but wonders how successful it will be if the owner/operator is the discard of Princess Rosa."

Cassie guessed those last words weren't from the magazine but rather were his own.

"Julian, that's ridiculous. Clientele as high-end as the ones we're trying to attract are sophisticated enough to see through this gibberish."

She could only hope she was telling the truth. But a seed of doubt and apprehension had settled in her chest, as well.

"I hope so. But she even questions my motives."

"Your motives? How so?"

He stared off into the distance, a look of utter disgust on his face at what he was about to tell her. "Given the demographics of our target market, she speculates that I'm doing this as a way to perhaps meet another woman on par with the princess I was supposed to marry."

Cassie couldn't hide her gasp. "That's absurd."

He nodded and swallowed. "I know that. And you know that. But her readers may not. This is a very respected travel publication throughout all of Europe. I have no idea why they published such a gossipy hit piece. But the fact remains that they did exactly that."

"But how can anyone give this any kind of credence?" It sounded like nothing more than a trashy gossip article as far as she was concerned.

"I don't know. At the worst, it will detract from our bookings. She cites a similar resort on the Caribbean that she says is probably a better option. It's less pricey also."

"I see. And at the best?"

"I'll have my hands full with overzealous single women who are only staying with us to prove the writer's point. Mainly, to see if I'm indeed trying to find my next relationship through a business venture."

That possibility had bile rising in Cassie's throat. The thought of beautiful well-heeled women throwing themselves at Julian left a sour taste in her mouth. As much as she wanted to deny it, she found that prospect more upsetting than the risk to bookings. How unprofessional of her.

"Which brings up all sorts of issues. Ethical and otherwise," Julian continued.

"Julian, this is so unfair. What can we do? There has to be something. Can we sue?"

"I suppose, but that's not going to help the Paraiso in any way." He rubbed a palm down his face. "I'm afraid I can only think of one solution under such short notice. But it will require quite a bit from you for it to work."

"What is it? I'll do anything, of course."

He shocked her by taking her hand into his. Then shocked her even more with his next words. "I think we should get married."

She couldn't have possibly heard him correctly. Could the aroma of sangria somehow make one tipsy if they hadn't so much as had one sip? That had to be what was happening here. Otherwise, the only alternative was that Julian had just proposed to her.

"I'm sorry. I could have sworn you just asked me to marry you." She took a sip of her juice midchuckle.

"That's exactly what I did," he answered her with a completely straight face. The man certainly had a believable delivery.

"Ha, ha. That's really funny, Julian."

He rubbed his chin as he studied her. "Funny?"

"Yes. But really. What are we going to do about this article?"

"I'm not trying to be funny, *bella*. I am asking you to marry me."

Cassie sucked in a breath and leaned back in her chair. "You're serious." This was really happening. Had he come to some sort of personal revelation? Had he concluded that they belonged together because they'd been hitting it off so well since first meeting? Aside from a few bumps and bruises, of course. She wasn't naive enough to think that Julian may have somehow miraculously fallen in love with her. Particularly after the happenings of last week. But maybe he'd grown to care her for just enough that he was entertaining the idea of marriage as compatible friends who had nothing to lose. Not terribly romantic but she'd always been a realist.

Her thoughts gave her pause. Was she really considering his suggestion? She no longer knew which one of them was being more ridiculous.

All she knew for certain was that her head was spinning.

"Yes. I am very serious," Julian continued. "It would be beneficial to both of us to become husband and wife. Nothing more than another business transaction like the one we entered into back in Boston."

Beneficial. Business transaction.

Those terms threw cold water on any fanciful thoughts she may have been entertaining about the two of them.

"I'm sorry, I'm just not following, Julian. What exactly are you suggesting? Some kind of marriage of convenience?"

"Precisely. Not a forever marriage. Just temporary. Maybe a year. Eighteen months at the most. That should be enough time to be fully established as an exclusive vacation spot."

Of all the ways Cassie had imagined being proposed to since she was a little girl, this particular scenario hadn't even crossed the far depths of her imagination. Though the setting and the man sitting across from her certainly fit the ideal, the rest of it made no sense at all. Plus, there was no mention of the one word every woman dreamed of hearing during such a moment. *Love.* Julian didn't love her. He may care for her and he may have taken steps to ensure she was healthy during this pregnancy, but he didn't love her in any way that mattered. And chances were, he never would. From what she could surmise, he still wasn't over the woman he'd been prepared to marry for real two years ago.

Not that she could blame him. It must be hard to try and get over a royal princess who'd left you at the altar.

She tried to laugh it all off. "That's preposterous. You're talking the stuff of movies and fiction novels."

"All fiction is based on reality. Wouldn't you agree?"

She leaned over the table. "Julian, you're worried about your business. I understand that. And you think you've found a solution. But this makes no sense. We can't get married so that your resort opening doesn't suffer."

He rubbed his eyes and exhaled a deep sigh. "You're right. Of course. It's just, when the idea popped into my head last night in bed, it made so much sense. In so many ways."

Despite herself, Cassie found herself curious to hear exactly what he'd been thinking. "What kind of ways?"

"Well, for one, it would squash any of the gossip or rumors an article such as this may lead to."

That was a debatable point. "I'm not so sure," she countered. "Isn't it a little too out of the blue? On the heels of this article?" She pointed to the screen.

Julian nodded. "You think people will see it as too convenient? An obvious response."

She nodded. He'd clearly thought of that himself.

"It's a risk," he admitted. "But I think skepticism will blow over in time. Especially once we're seen together out and about."

He leaned in closer to her, a hint of mischief twinkled in his eyes. "You have to admit, we have observable chemistry. People are bound to see it."

She wasn't sure how to respond to that declaration. He'd not only noticed the sparks between them, he was acknowledging them.

"Besides, maybe the author has a point," Julian added.

Cassie blinked at him in surprise. "Come again?"

"Even I have to admit that the concept of a female exclusive resort makes more sense if its CEO is a family man."

"Family?"

"You are pregnant, *bella*." he said, amusement twinkling in his eyes. As if she'd forgotten.

"Yes. By another man."

"That's true. A man who wants nothing to do with you or the baby."

Ouch. True though his blunt statement was,

it still hurt to hear it out loud. More so that the words came from Julian's mouth.

Julian continued. "I would take full responsibility for the child. He or she is my adopted niece or nephew, after all."

"I see." They were the only two words she could muster. Her brain was a mishmash of scattered thoughts.

"The child doesn't have to call me Father. We can talk about exactly how I'm presented once they're old enough. But I'll be there for whatever he or she may need. Whenever they may need. Even after our so-called marriage is over."

He meant it, she knew. Julian was committing to her child as a parental figure this very moment. Even if he had no intention of genuinely committing to Cassie.

"You're asking for a year, huh?" she asked, for clarification. "After that, my baby and I will be free to head back to America if we want to?"

His eyes darkened before he nodded. "That's correct. If that is what you wish."

"Why?"

"Why what?"

"Why would I agree to this?"

He reached for her hand once more. Warmth from his skin seeped through hers and sent a longing through her center. How elated she would feel if any of this were real. "Think about it, Cassie. You would be giving your child a name, a chance to become part of the family they belong to."

His words were so very tempting. A family was all she'd ever really longed for, what she desperately wanted for her child. To belong, to be a part of a loving unit. Like the one Julian, his mother, his brothers and even the staff at the resort exemplified.

Julian continued to press his case. "If you marry me, the child will be a Santigo in every sense. Entitled to all the privileges and rights to the family businesses. For the rest of his or her life." He gave her hand a squeeze. "And I vow, that no matter what happens at the end of a year, I will always be a fixture in this child's life. Like I said, the child is essentially my niece or nephew. I intend to be involved in any way I can as they grow up."

A father figure. The one thing she couldn't give her child on her own, no matter how hard she tried. She knew Julian would be true to his word. He'd never turn his back on her baby if he was giving her his vow right now. Still, the whole concept seemed so far-fetched.

"What about your mother? The rest of the family? Or Carlos, for that matter? What will you tell them all?"

"You leave them for me to deal with."

Cassie squeezed her eyes shut and tried to think. What Julian was proposing made perfect sense on the surface. Her child would be taken care of, would be legitimately included in the family he or she was technically a part of. Would it be fair for her to deprive her baby of such an opportunity?

The answer was clear. She forced her trepidation away and followed her gut. "Okay. I'll do it. I'll marry you."

To her surprise once more, Julian reached over the table and took her lips with his own. Before she knew it, she was being thoroughly kissed in such a way that she lost all sense of reality. The taste of him took her breath away.

When he broke away, the smile he gave her melted her heart even more.

He called the server over and handed him his phone. "Please take a picture of us." Cassie wasn't naive enough to think Julian was really looking to capture the occasion in any way. She had a sneaking suspicion the photo would end up online in a featured website spread before the night was over. She swallowed past the disappointment. It would be silly to look too deeply into this sham marriage. As Julian said, it was merely another business agreement between them.

"Of course, sir," the waiter responded, taking the phone and aiming it in their direction. "Special occasion?"

"Yes," Julian answered. "We've just gotten engaged."

CHAPTER THIRTEEN

HE'D BEEN THINKING about it since that day at the ruins. Wasn't even sure he was going to do it up until that very moment. The article had helped solidify Julian's decision.

Oh, he knew very well that proposing was a rather unconventional way to address Cassie's predicament. But it made sense if one analyzed all the variables. A marriage of convenience, as she'd described it, gave Cassie an out if she wanted to say no. And truthfully, the marriage would in fact be a good rebuttal for the trashy article in that blasted travel magazine.

All very logical, very thought-out. His feelings toward Cassie had nothing to do with his proposal of a sham marriage. None whatsoever. He was simply being practical in a way that made sense for them both.

They found his mother and Safina both in the kitchen, sampling some kind of stew that filled the entire room with the scent of tomato and spices. A stroke of luck, Julian figured. This way, they'd be able to make the announcement to both at once.

"We have some news, Mother. Safina." He nodded to his chef, a friend he'd known for close to ten years, practically part of the family.

He pulled Cassie close to his side. "Show them."

She was shaking where she stood. Hopefully, the other women wouldn't notice. Hesitantly, she lifted her hand to show them the ring he'd stopped for at a jewelry store in town on their way back.

Maria clasped a hand to her mouth. Safina tore off her chef's hat and tossed it in the air with a boisterous laugh.

"Dios! Felicidades, mi niño!"

His mother took Cassie's face between her palms and gave her a kiss on each cheek.

"Gracias," Cassie responded with a perfect Spanish accent, accelerating the glee on Maria's face.

Safina had reached their side as well and

had hugged both him and Cassie at least three times already.

The utter joy on the two women's faces had guilt twisting in his center. He knew this was the right thing to do, this fake marriage. But he couldn't help but feel bitter disappointment that it had to be pretend. In another life, Cassie would be the exact type of woman he would happily marry for real. She was talented, a dedicated mother to the child she carried. Though worlds different from Rosa, he found he was attracted to her in a way that felt more authentic, more heartfelt.

With Rosa, he never knew who he was going to wake up next to—the entitled princess, the rebellious youngest daughter of a noble family or the myriad personalities in between. Cassie was Cassie. Whether it made sense or not, he felt as if he'd known her for much longer than the month or so since he'd first walked into her apartment.

He didn't recall ever feeling like he actually knew Rosa. The true Rosa.

"We'll have to tell everyone right away," his mother was saying. "Your brothers first, of course. Then your aunt and uncle and cousins in Madrid. Everyone else."

"I'll start making a list," Safina offered.

"I wish your father were here to see this," his mother said, giving Cassie another hug, then embracing him again tightly.

Julian cringed at her words. If his *padre* was up there watching, he knew exactly how he was deceiving Maria. He uttered a silent prayer of forgiveness to the parent he'd lost years ago.

"I knew it," his mother declared. "I knew from the moment I walked into that hallway that first day that you two were going to end up together."

"And I knew it when I watched him feed her oysters. Before you even arrived, Maria," Safina added, as if the two women were competing for who'd figured it out first.

Little did they know.

"Tell us everything," Safina said, leading them to the large wooden table at the side of the room and pulling out four chairs. "How did Julian propose?"

Cassie's smile hadn't faltered a bit. Actually, her lips hadn't so much as moved since they'd walked in here. In fact, she was smiling so widely, he worried she might end up with a strained jaw before the day was over.

Julian felt a moment of self-loathing. At least he'd had some time to prepare for this. He cleared his throat, ready to answer the question in her stead. If it would help to ease some of her discomfort, he'd be happy to speak for her until this whole charade was over.

He should have known better. Cassie visibly squared her shoulders and appeared to get a hold of herself. "Well, it was really quite romantic," she began. "First, he took me to the botanical garden and showed me the majestic plants and cacti."

"Oh! That's lovely."

"We took a walk around the man-made lake and admired the bamboo trees. Some of them are works of art."

"Did you suspect anything?" Safina asked.

Cassie winked at her conspiratorially and squeezed Julian's knee. Electricity shot through his leg at her touch. "I didn't suspect a thing. Get this, he told me it was a business outing to check out an excursion spot.

He planned the surprise perfectly. I didn't see any of it coming."

She turned to flash him a smile full of meaning. It occurred to him she hadn't told a single lie.

Safina dotted her eyes with a thick kitchen towel. His mother appeared teary too. He hadn't realized how much these two women had grown to love Cassie, as well.

As well?

He didn't have time to analyze that thought. Cassie continued to describe the afternoon. With a genius sense of storytelling, she relayed the events as if Julian had spent countless hours planning the perfect proposal. When in reality, he'd taken her on a business trip then dropped a crazy idea on her lap unexpectedly during lunch.

He liked her version of the proposal so much better.

Cassie hadn't actually been expecting the call to go through. She'd been trying to call regularly with no luck for the past few days, since Julian had "proposed." So she was pleasantly surprised when Zara's voice came on the line after the second ring.

"Hey. You're finally in a spot with cell service."

"Cassie!"

"Hello, BFF."

"I probably won't have service for long," her friend said with a note of urgency. "We need to catch up fast. How are you? And the baby?"

"Fine. We're both doing fine."

"I'm still the prime candidate for godmother, right? I better be."

Cassie had to laugh at the seriousness in Zara's tone. "Who else?"

"Good. There is no one else."

"No, there isn't. I assure you."

"What have you been up to on the lovely isle of Mallorca? Are you exploring and trying all sorts of new experiences?" Zara wanted to know. "Is it everything you'd hoped it would be?"

If only her friend could guess what a loaded question she'd just asked. "It's such an adventure, Zara. The resort itself, all the sites. Did the photos I emailed you of the Roman ruins come through?"

"They did and they're absolutely lovely. You look beautiful in them. Pregnancy suits you."

Cassie curled deeper into the sofa in her suite and simply reveled in hearing the sound of her dear friend's voice. She missed Zara more than she would have guessed. Thank God a call had finally gone through.

"And your boss!" Zara suddenly exclaimed.

"What about him?"

"Hubba-hubba. That man looks way too tempting in khakis and a V-neck. You can't tell me you haven't noticed."

Here it was. Cassie figured it was as good a segue as any. "Speaking of Julian, there's something I wanted to tell you."

Zara didn't respond, simply waited for her to speak.

Cassie had to clear her throat before she could continue. "It so happens we're engaged to be married."

Zara's gasp was clear as a bell. Followed by yet more silence. So long that Cassie began to wonder if the connection had failed or if she'd simply rendered her friend speechless. Apparently, it was the latter. Finally, Zara's voice came through loud and clear.

"What! I could have sworn you just said you're getting married! To Julian!"

"I did indeed."

"You're serious?"

Cassie had to stifle the urge to giggle. "Yes."

The flurry of questions started then. "When? How did this happen? How much time do I have to clear my schedule so that I can be there? How can I—"

It was hard for Cassie to get a word in. Finally, Zara stopped to take a breath and she managed to jump in. "You don't have to clear your schedule, Zara. The wedding is scheduled to take place in two weeks. But it's not going to be a real wedding. Or a real marriage."

That seemed to give her pause. "Come again?"

Cassie sighed. "It's a long story."

"Start talking, then. Fast."

Any amusement she felt waned quickly as she tried to figure out a way to explain it all.

She decided on simply telling Zara the truth as best she could. "It's not real."

"Huh?"

"It's for his business."

"Now you've really lost me."

Cassie knew she was making a mess of this conversation. But how exactly did one explain a modern-day marriage of convenience?

She gave it another try. "To ensure a successful opening. I'll explain fully when I see you. It's impossible to do it over the phone."

Cassie could imagine the utter confusion that was no doubt running through Zara's head at the moment.

"Are you telling me that you're getting married as part of some kind of business interest? That's insane, Wells!"

"Crazy or not, it happens to be the truth."

Again, her words were met with yet more silence.

"Are you still there, Zara?"

Zara answered right away. "Yes. I'm just trying to grasp what you've told me. I know I've asked this before, but are you sure you haven't taken up fiction writing in your spare time?"

Heavens. This was harder to explain than Cassie had imagined it would be. "Suffice it to say the marriage will be a sham. Fake."

"Huh," her friend simply responded.

"I know it's a lot."

"It really is. 'Cause I'm still staring at these photos you sent of the two of you at that archaeological site."

"And?"

"And the way that man is looking at you, in every single shot, is about as real as it gets."

The forty-eight hours preceding her scheduled wedding seemed to be going by in a blurry haze. Sleep was eluding her and she could hardly focus when she tried to get any work done. She could only hope she was doing the right thing. Because it was much too late to back out now.

For at least the next year or so, she would become Mrs. Julian Santigo. Her child would have a legitimate name. In complete contrast to what Carlos had offered her, Julian wanted to be a part of her child's life. Whereas Carlos's offer of financial security was essentially a payout to keep them both out of his hair, Julian vowed to stay in her child's life regardless of what happened in the future.

All it would take was participating in a fake marriage.

She felt Julian's presence behind her in the kitchen before she saw him. She'd been picking at an omelet for the better part of twenty minutes, her appetite completely noncooperative. The egg had grown cold and even less appealing but she was determined to eat at least a few bites to try and keep her energy up.

Julian approached her from behind. "I guess we're really going through with this," she said, studying her hands. The heavy, brilliant diamond sitting on her left ring finger still felt foreign and out of place.

"That we are, *bella*," Julian responded, taking a seat next to her at the counter. "No one but the two of us needs to know it's a complete farce."

She cringed internally at the word. Maybe Julian being a non-native English speaker hadn't realized how harsh that word sounded. Not that he was wrong. The first, and maybe the only, wedding of her life would be a fake one. A spectacle. One that would have plenty of participants. Countless members of Julian's family had flown in over the past couple of days from every corner of the earth to help them celebrate. Yet others were still at this very moment making their way to the resort from all over Europe to participate in the upcoming nuptials. The whole clan was due to eat lunch together on the beach later to officially begin the festivities before the big day.

Thankfully there was no sign of Carlos. Cassie had to assume Julian had made certain his cousin knew not to make an appearance.

"I suppose I better go get ready for the day, then," she announced and stood.

"I suppose so. My mother is waiting for you to speak beforehand. Some wedding details she wants to go over."

Cassie sighed with resignation. She appreciated the enthusiasm from Julian's mother, she really did. But there was just so much hovering. Not only from Maria but Safina, as well. Even Larrisa, the nurse, was often around asking about ways she might be able to help.

So much for taking a quick nap first. She really was feeling rather run-down after a restless night of sleep. On top of the pregnancy and the constant need to keep up the pretense of a happily engaged couple, Cassie felt as if her energy was draining away like a spent battery.

Luckily it would all be over soon. Though, if she were being honest with herself, she would have to admit that this was simply the beginning. After the ceremony in two days, she'd be committed to spending at least a year pretending to be something she wasn't—a cherished wife. Something she might very well never be in this lifetime.

Regardless of what Zara thought she saw in those photos, Julian was doing this for the sake of his business, to get the resort off the ground. And she was doing it for the sake of her unborn child. But she'd come to a realization over the past few days after they'd announced their so-called "announcement." At every turn, every moment, they'd had to pretend to be in love; every time Julian had kissed her, Cassie had wanted all of it to be real. There was no denying it.

What exactly was she setting her heart up for here?

She wanted him to feel electricity the same way she did every time he touched her. She wanted him to be excited about reciting vows to her as they stood before all of his relatives. She'd had a dream last night that he'd actually laughed at her as she approached where he stood in the chapel while she walked down the aisle. Even though it wasn't real, only a dream, she'd woken up with tears streaming down her face.

Because none of it was real.

And it hurt because she loved him. She'd fully accepted that now. Somehow, she'd fallen head over heels in love with a man who saw her as nothing more than a pregnant woman he needed for a business venture.

An insane, naive part of her wanted to tell him all that and more. Of course, she wouldn't. Instead she walked slowly to the door to leave him until their fake wedding.

A sudden ripple of movement shifted around in her stomach. It took a second for Cassie to realize what she was experiencing.

"Oh!"

Julian was by her side in an instant. "Cassie? What is it? Are you all right?"

She didn't answer right away, simply took his hand and placed it on her stomach where she felt the twinge, willing for there to be more where that came from. It took a couple minutes but finally it happened again right in the same spot. Julian's head snapped up in surprise.

"Is that—?"

She nodded with all the glee she felt surge through her. "Yes. The baby is kicking. This is the first time."

Julian grinned wide and kept his hand in place. To her delight, the baby kicked again. "It's almost as if the little tyke is congratulating us."

Cassie laughed out loud in pleasure. The sensation was unlike anything she'd felt before. All these weeks, she'd intrinsically known that she was carrying a life inside her. But to feel it so physically took her breath away.

Julian seemed as enthralled by it as she was.

They stood that way for a while, just savoring the moment, anticipating it happening again and waiting with bated breath.

A shadow fell suddenly over the open doorway. A masculine voice sounded in the next instant. An all-too-familiar voice that had Cassie's blood running cold in her veins.

"Hola, mi primo."

CHAPTER FOURTEEN

"Hello, cousin."

Julian didn't have to turn around to know exactly who stood in the doorway. He'd never mistake who that voice belonged to. He bit out a vicious curse before dropping his hand from Cassie's midsection.

To her credit, Cassie stood still and calm, not betraying any kind of emotion. But her eyes were wide and full of shock.

"Cassie," Carlos added. An insane urge to throttle the man nearly overtook Julian where he stood—simply because he'd dared to utter her name. Funny, he'd never considered himself to be the jealous type. But now, with the father of Cassie's baby standing there in his doorway, Julian realized just how possessive he could be.

Julian gave her hand a reassuring squeeze. "Are you here to congratulate us, then, Carlos?"

"I need to speak to you, Julian. Alone."

Julian hesitated. The last thing he wanted was to deal with his problematic cousin right now, given what his presence must ultimately mean. But what choice did he have?

"Would you please excuse us, Cassie?" he asked, reluctantly releasing her hand.

Cassie's eyes grew wide with panic. "It'll be okay," he said softly against her ear. "I'll come get you in a few minutes."

She gave him the slightest nod before turning to leave. He felt no small amount of satisfaction that she walked past Carlos without so much as glancing in his direction. His cousin's grimace said her snub hadn't gone unnoticed.

Julian feigned a calmness he didn't feel as he sat back down. He motioned for Carlos to take the chair across the table from him.

"What can I do for you, Carlos?" he asked as the other man sat down. Now that he was closer, Julian noticed a number of bruises along his face. He sported an angry cut above his right eye. "And what in heaven's name happened to your face?"

"The answer to that is the reason I'm here."

Julian tapped the table between them. What game was Carlos playing? Had he been in some kind of fight as a result of his gambling habits? Perhaps he was here looking for money in return for keeping quiet about the baby. If that was the case, Julian would happily pay any amount.

"I'm sure we can come to a mutually satisfactory agreement. Did you have a figure in mind?" he asked.

Carlos huffed out a laugh. "Believe it or not, it's not money I'm after. Not this time."

His words sent alarm bells ringing through Julian's head. "Then what? I'm afraid I don't have a lot of time here. Can we just cut to the chase? Why exactly are you here? And what does it have to do with the fact that your face is completely banged up?"

"I was in a boating accident about two weeks ago. It's why I haven't been answering your attempts to get a hold of me."

"I see. Are you all right?"

"I am now. But it was touch and go there for a while. Some internal bleeding that could have resulted in a much different result. Luckily, the doctors in France were able to cauterize the affected organ."

"I'm glad you're okay," Julian said and fully meant it. Good or bad, for all practical purposes, Carlos was family. They'd grown up together. He'd just chosen a much different path in life. One filled with adventure and risk-taking that sometimes led to dangerous outcomes. Like speedboat accidents off the coast of France.

Or leaving vulnerable women behind when they were pregnant with his child.

"So why exactly are you here, then?" Julian asked again. "Why did you travel all this way when you could have easily sent me an email or text to tell me all this?"

"I saw your wedding announcement from my hospital bed, cousin. I thought maybe my concussion was having me see things. Because there it was in black and white. You were engaged to marry Cassandra."

"And?"

"Let's just say it came as a bit of a shock."

Julian had to give him that. In his defense, he'd been trying to reach Carlos before he had to find out the way he had. He'd also been warning him not to show up here. Precisely to avoid the scenario before them now.

"Were you expecting Cassie to stay unattached? You did leave her, after all. Alone and pregnant with your unborn child."

Carlos characteristically shrugged that off. "I'll tell you what I didn't expect. That my cousin, who I simply asked to hand deliver an envelope to her, would end up her fiancé."

He waited a beat before going on.

"In any case, I came to some realizations after the accident," Carlos continued. Something about his tone made the hair at the back of Julian's neck stand up.

"Realizations?"

His cousin nodded.

"I realized just how short life could be. Which in turn made me realize what's truly important."

Julian didn't need to hear any more to know where this was going and the understanding sent a chill of trepidation down his spine. Carlos's next words confirmed what he'd been dreading.

"I want to be a part of my child's life, Julian. I have a right to be that baby's father."

Julian had no argument for that. For Carlos was right. But there was so much more to the story here. "And what of Cassie?"

Carlos's eyes narrowed. "I think I could ask you that, as well."

"What exactly is that supposed to mean?"

"You're ready to marry her when you met her just few weeks ago? Am I supposed to believe the two of you suddenly fell in love? Enough to get married?"

Carlos may have been a jet-setting partyer without much regard to other people's needs, but he'd never been stupid.

"Why are you really doing this, Julian? Is it because you want to forget about Rosa finally?"

Julian didn't hesitate with his response. "Absolutely not."

"Then why?"

"I have my reasons."

Carlos's smirk of satisfaction told him he'd made a crucial mistake with his answer. A mistake he realized right away. But it was too late. The wrong words were already out. He hadn't thought to say he was marrying her out of love.

Julian had fallen into a trap completely of his own making. The truth was he did love her, had realized it long ago. He just hadn't been able to admit it. Not even to himself.

"I may have left her before but I'm here now," Carlos added. "And I have every right to be here. You can't deny me that."

Julian wanted to grab his cousin by the collar and yank him up out of the chair. Then he wanted to haul him unceremoniously out the door and demand he never show his face to either him or Cassie ever again.

But that was not the solution. Because as much as it pained him and tore him to shreds inside, he knew Carlos was right. He had a right to be that baby's father and become a part of his or her life.

But he had no right whatsoever to the woman Julian loved.

CHAPTER FIFTEEN

It took every ounce of control Julian possessed when he spoke to keep his voice steady and calm. Inside he was a storm of fury and ire. He'd never much liked the man his adopted cousin had become. But he'd never outright despised him. He was perilously close to doing so now.

"You may be the father, Carlos, but I'm Cassie's fiancé. We are due to be married in less than two days. Nothing you can do or say will change that."

Carlos didn't seem moved. "Then let's prove that."

"What's that supposed to mean?"

"I'd like to talk to Cassie. I want to hear exactly what she has to say."

Julian pinched the bridge of his nose. The sooner Carlos left, the sooner he and Cassie could get on with plans for their wedding. And plans for the rest of their lives.

"You can't keep me from speaking with the mother of my child," Carlos pressed.

As much as it pained him, Julian had to admit he had a point. But it wasn't his decision. "Whether you speak to Cassie or not is completely up to her."

"I'm part of her life, Julian. Hers and her child's. And I will be forever."

The words landed as viciously as any physical blows. Carlos hadn't said anything Julian didn't know. But Carlos meant he was staking his claim as the father of Cassie's child. A fact Julian would not be able to change.

"I merely want to establish expectations, Julian. With Cassie. I want her to know I'm ready to be a father. And to see what she has to say about moving forward given that fact."

Julian had half a mind to ignore everything but his desire to physically lift Carlos by the shoulders and haul him out the door. As good as that would feel, in the end it would solve nothing.

"Again. It's completely Cassie's decision whether she speaks with you or not."

Carlos shrugged, seemingly unconcerned. "I'll wait here while you ask her."

* * *

Cassie was a bundle of nerves by the time she heard Julian's knock on her door about an hour later. When she greeted him, she was ready to fling herself into his arms. What exactly did Carlos want? Why was he here?

But Julian's entire demeanor told her to hold back. He was distant, aloof. His expression sent a wave of alarm through her entire being. She forced herself to keep from going to him.

"I think you should speak with him," he told her before even uttering so much as a hello.

"I really don't see why."

"He's the father, Cassie. Neither one of us can deny that."

She couldn't believe what she was hearing. She was due to marry this man in less than forty-eight hours. But here he was, encouraging her to give someone else another chance. Someone who had betrayed her in the worst possible way. Was this some kind of family loyalty between the two men? If so, where exactly did that leave her? As a pawn to be toyed with at their will? If Julian really thought that, he had a surprise coming his way. She had more pride than that. Much more. "He turned his back on us."

"I know. But he swears he now wants to be a part of the child's life."

A little too late as far as she was concerned. "And you think that's fine? After all these weeks when he didn't even bother to check how I or his baby were managing?"

He rubbed his forehead. To his credit, he looked utterly miserable. Dark circles had appeared under his eyes and his hair was in complete disarray, as if he'd relentlessly run his fingers through it. "Of course not. But it's not up to me to deny him that."

"Well, it is up to me."

He nodded. "You're right. And if you want me to, I'll make him leave. But we both know he's very likely to come back."

She hated that he was right. "Why did he change his mind? After all this time?" For the life of her, she couldn't figure it out.

"He's been involved in some kind of accident. I'll let Carlos explain all that for himself."

She felt her lip tremble and willed some

semblance of self-control. How was this even happening? She'd known all along that Julian didn't truly love her. But she'd been trying to fool herself into thinking he may have developed some feelings toward her at the very least.

Had he only proposed to her out of a sense of obligation? To help her with the baby? And now that the real father was here, was he was reconsidering?

"I just don't want you to regret anything later, Cass. Your baby has a right to know his or her real father."

Cass. That was new. He'd never called her that before. She wasn't sure how to take the new development. Everything about him was different. As if she'd never even known the man she had almost married. Even if it was to be a completely fake marriage of convenience.

"Why did you ask me to marry you, Julian? The truth."

She wanted to hear him explain, once and for all, what his reasoning was. The real reasons. His true motivation. She stopped breathing as she waited for him to respond.

"We discussed all the reasons when I proposed, *bella*. Don't you remember?"

Her heart shattered at his nonanswer. He couldn't say it. He couldn't tell her that he cared for her, that he wanted to be a part of her and her baby's life. Simple words that would have meant so much and that might have changed everything.

That was it, she couldn't take any more. She'd been so naive all this time. Assuming that even if he didn't love her, she might still mean something to him. It was clear now that she'd never been more than an employee. A means to an end.

Now that Carlos was back, he would probably find a different way to address the business concern this marriage was supposed to fix. He had no real need for her.

Well, no more. She would cut her losses and leave. She'd fulfilled enough of her business duties that technically she'd earned the advance he'd already wired her, as far as she was concerned. As for the rest, it wasn't worth her pride nor her soul. All her life she'd struggled to achieve what she wanted;

she could do the same for both her and her child now.

"I think I'd like to be alone."

"Cassie—"

She held a hand up to stop him. She didn't need to hear any more. Couldn't bear to. There was really nothing more to say between them. Everything was crystal clear.

She walked over to the door and held it open for him. "Please leave, Julian." The years she'd spent being tossed from foster home to foster home, all the promises her mother had made only to break them at the first temptation, all those experiences had made her vow that she would ensure better for her child. There really was no choice to be made here, regardless of what Julian said.

She refused to look him in the eye as he walked out.

Maria was waiting for him when he returned to the resort lobby. As much as he loved his mother, Julian was really in no mood for chitchat right now.

"We missed you at lunch," she informed

him. "Neither you nor Cassie were anywhere to be found."

"I'm sorry, Mama. I'll be sure to apologize to everyone. I'm sure Safina's excellent meal made up for our absence."

"Never mind the food," his mother responded. "We were all worried about you. Is everything all right?"

"Please let everyone know everything is fine. We just weren't terribly hungry, that's all." He tried to step aside her to make his way to the office but she just matched his step, blocking his path.

"I have some work to do," Julian said as he tried to sidestep her once more, only to be impeded the same way.

"Not until you tell me what's happening," Maria insisted. "Why did you two really miss the family lunch? And was that Carlos I saw earlier? I thought no one had heard from him. Is he all right?"

There was nothing for it. Maria wasn't going to leave him alone until she had some answers.

He motioned for her to follow him into his office.

"What's really going on?" Maria pressed before he'd even had a chance to close his door.

He pulled out a chair for her to sit, then plopped down on his own across from her at his desk.

"Carlos is here because he's the father."

He watched the transformation on her face as the full impact of his words sunk in. Maria clasped a hand over her mouth. *"Ay, Dios!"*

"He's the only reason I met Cassie in Boston. He wanted me to deliver a…compensation to her…but made it clear to her that he wanted nothing to do with the baby."

"That no-good— Where is he?" she demanded. "He's not too old for a good ear twisting from his *tia.*"

Julian had no doubt she'd deliver said twisting as soon as Maria found her adopted nephew. But first things first. "The point is, he's changed his mind."

"Changed his mind in what way?"

"About being a real father to the baby."

Maria narrowed her eyes on him. "The baby is one thing. No one has the right to deny a father who wants to be part of a child's life.

But I'm sure you told him what's what as far as Cassie is concerned. She's your fiancée."

Julian pinched the bridge of his nose. If only things were as black-and-white as Maria believed.

"It's not that simple, Mama."

Maria's lips tightened. That was never a good sign. His mother was clearly reaching the end of her patience with him. "What exactly are you saying, son?" Julian's silence was all the answer she needed. She let loose a string of Spanish curses that would have shocked his dear departed *padre*.

"What is the matter with you? You're marrying Cassie in less than two days!"

He really had no desire to get into the whole marriage-of-convenience thing with her right now. "It's complicated. At the very least, I think they need to talk."

His mother glared at him, incredulous. "Carlos is not the only one who needs an ear twisting. You two will need to take turns."

"He's the father of her child."

"And you're the man who loves her."

When she stated it so plainly that way, Julian had to seriously weigh the words. Fake betrothal or not, he couldn't deny any longer the truth of Maria's statement. Still, none of that changed the underlying facts.

Maria's eyes softened. "I see. This is about Rosa more than it is about Cassie. You want to see exactly what she'll do."

Was that what he was doing? Was he waiting to see if Cassie would prove herself? He didn't even know anymore.

"It's about not making the same mistake twice," he countered. But his words rang hollow even to his own ears. The one thing he knew for sure was that he'd be lost without Cassandra Wells in his life. He couldn't imagine waking up tomorrow and not having her be a part of his future.

What had he done?

He should have followed his instincts and tossed Carlos out on his behind the moment he'd shown up regardless of his status as the baby's father. He should have insisted revisiting any custodial arrangement *after* he and Cassie were married. It was all so clear now, he wanted to kick himself for not seeing it sooner. Much sooner.

"I'm so sad to find out I've raised a fool

for a son," Maria interrupted his regretful thoughts, slowly shaking her head.

Ouch. His mother had never been one to spare feelings when she felt the matter was important enough. This time cut a bit deeper than in the past though. Because she was completely right. He'd behaved like a fool. All for the sake of his pride.

She didn't give him a chance to respond. "Rosa was nothing like Cassie, *mi niño*. She only loved herself. Cassie is in love with you. I know you realize that deep in your heart."

"Does Cassie?"

She shrugged. "Well, how did she react at Carlos's return?"

Julian looked off into the distance. "Not well. Not even a little bit."

"Then why are you still sitting here? For heaven's sake. We have a wedding to prepare for."

With that she slapped her hands to her jean-clad thighs and sprung up out of her chair.

"Where are you going?" Julian asked her.

"To find my nephew and deliver that ear twisting." She pointed her manicured finger at him. "And you're going to find your bride.

Before it's too late. Don't let Rosa hurt you any more than she has already. It takes more than biology to make a family. You will make an excellent father. I know that in my soul. I get the feeling Cassie does too."

His mother was a wise woman. One who hadn't often been wrong as far as he'd witnessed.

He stood and walked over to where she sat, gave her a peck on the cheek. "Gracias, Mama."

"De nada," she answered, cupping his chin affectionately.

"Try to go easy on Carlos when you find him," he told her. "He's had a rough couple of weeks."

She was gone when he went to find her. Her suite empty, nothing of hers remained. The only item she'd left behind was the engagement ring he'd given her, wrapped up in its original velvet box and sitting on the center coffee table. She would have had every right to take it if she'd chosen to. Perhaps she wanted nothing at all whatsoever to do with him. She could hardly be blamed for feeling that way.

Julian paced back and forth, searching for some kind of answer as to where she might have gone. Dialing her number sent him directly to a voice mail box. He left three long-winded messages before the automated voice told him her box was full.

Mallorca was a large island and she could be anywhere. Hell, for all he knew she'd somehow booked a last-minute seat and was on an airplane back to the States right this minute.

That possibility had bile churning in his gut. The thought that she might be on her way across the world.

He would have no one but himself to blame if he couldn't find her. Now that he'd finally found the courage to admit what she meant to him, it appeared to be too late. He walked over to the balcony and slammed his fist against the sliding glass door.

He'd blown it. Like a fool he'd let go of something precious and rare simply because he'd been too scared. He'd ensured the utter definition of a self-fulfilling prophecy, bringing about the very thing he feared the most.

In this case, losing the one woman he'd ever truly loved.

His phone vibrated in his pocket with an incoming message. With hasty fingers, he pulled it out and called up the email app.

Sure enough, it was from Cassie.

Please send my deepest, sincerest apologies to everyone who has arrived on the island to attend the wedding. I simply cannot bring myself to go through with it. As much as I want to be your wife, I guess I'm not fully prepared to accept the fact that it isn't ever going to be real. I feel it's important to admit that to you now.

I should have never accepted your proposal, Julian. Because I knew deep down that even a fake marriage would have meant more to me than it ever would have for you.

I have never before reneged on an agreement but feel this time I truly have no choice but to back out.

You will always be in my heart. But for the sake of my child, as well as myself, I need to move on.

I hope you understand.

He typed out a response and hit Send. Then waited with anticipation, willing the ding of an incoming message to sound once again. He lost track of how long he just stood there staring at the small screen before he gave up.

Julian flung the device so hard against the wall, he heard the glass shatter. He understood all right. He understood exactly how much of a fool he'd been to not see what was clearly in front of him all this time.

The second Carlos even hinted at asking Cassie for a second chance, he should have shown the other man out the door. He'd pretended his failure to do so had some basis in nobility or decency on his part. But he'd been lying to himself. His motive had been purely based on fear.

And now he would have to pay for it. He'd had a chance at some real happiness with a woman who loved him and a child he would have cherished. Like a fool, he'd walked away from it all. He would never forgive himself.

He could only hope that someday Cassie might.

* * *

Cassie checked inside her carry-on bag one more time for all the essentials before calling up her electronic boarding pass on her smartphone. The plane would be boarding soon. She had a long day of travel in front of her that she wasn't looking forward to.

Her heart still felt heavy, her eyes still stung from all the tears she'd shed. She'd come to love this island. And even though she'd arrived all those weeks ago knowing none of this was to be permanent, she still felt as if she was leaving a piece of herself behind. Part of her soul would always belong here. And part of her heart would always belong to Julian.

She would try to move on with her life just as she expected him to. Another princess or debutante or supermodel was most likely even now waiting in the wings. No doubt one day she'd read about it just as she would read about the success of the Paraiso in the travel magazines. She had no doubt the resort would indeed be a major success. Julian would see to it.

At least she could say she'd had some small role in getting it there.

Walking through the terminal, she thought she caught a whiff of the now so familiar cologne that she'd come to closely associate with Julian. Great, now she was imagining his scent. As if it wasn't bad enough that man constantly haunted her dreams both day and night.

She would have been married in a few short hours if things had gone according to plan. But instead, she was here about to board a plane back home to Boston after spending the past day and a half in a small hotel by the airport.

There it was again. Julian's cologne. Either pregnancy was making her imagination much more vivid or someone here in the airport lounge wore the same scent that Julian sported.

A hand gently touched her shoulder and she realized there was yet another possibility. Almost afraid to know for certain, Cassie took a deep breath and closed her eyes before turning around.

Her heart leaped in her chest when she

opened them again. It really was Julian standing before her.

He looked completely disheveled and unkempt. Part of his shirt was untucked, his hair fell in unruly curls over his forehead. He clearly hadn't shaved in at least a day.

He was stunningly, breathtakingly handsome.

"Hola."

"Julian, what are you doing here?" The question came out in a breathless gasp. Her shock had rendered her nearly speechless.

"What do you think I'm doing here? I'm bringing you back home."

That made no sense. Pregnant or not, she didn't need someone to accompany her back to Boston. How hapless did he think she was? That would be a complete waste of time for him, unless he had some type of business there. Judging by his appearance, that wasn't the case.

"I can get to Boston without a guide. I hope you haven't bought any kind of ticket."

He blinked at her. "What are you talking about? I'm bringing you home. Back to the Paraiso. Where you belong."

Something fluttered in the pit of her stomach and traveled upward toward her heart. Definitely not the baby kicking, though there'd been a fair amount of that going on since yesterday, as well.

Julian reached for her bag. "Can we go, please? I've been sitting here since yesterday and I'd really like to get back and take a nice long shower."

Cassie was too stunned to move. He'd been here all night? He intended to bring her back to the resort?

"Julian, please tell me what's going on. Why in the world have you been here all night?"

He practically rolled his eyes at her. "Because there was more than one flight to Boston and I didn't want to miss the one you were on."

She stared at him blankly.

He continued, "Because I love you. I might have loved you since the day you set your kitchen on fire."

She couldn't help it. Her body and her mind simply refused to move. It was as if she were outside of herself watching all this play out. But whoo, boy, once those emotional floodgates opened up, she wasn't sure how in the world she'd be able to contain them. This was really happening. Julian was really here telling her he loved her.

Julian huffed out a breath. "Fine, I wasn't really planning on doing this here. Lord knows you deserve a better one this time, but here goes…" Then to her utter shock, he dropped to one knee onto the ground before her. Several passersby stopped in their tracks to stare. Every muscle in Cassie's frame remained completely frozen.

She stood stone-still as Julian pulled a small object out of his pants pocket and took her hand. The ring.

Only it wasn't the ring he'd purchased in haste the day of their trip to the botanical garden. This one was a simpler band with a smaller, oval cut stone. "This belonged to my grandmother. I'd like you to have it. To wear it as my wife." He slipped it on her trembling finger. "Cassie Wells, please say you'll do me the honor of marrying me."

Cassie wasn't sure how she managed it but she finally found her voice. "Oh, Julian." She pulled him up and threw her arms around his neck, inhaling the scent of him, savoring the feel of his skin.

"Is that a yes?" he asked, nuzzling her neck "We can get married today as planned or we can do it next week or a year from now or right after the baby comes. I don't care. Whenever you want, *mi bella*." He squeezed her tighter up against him. "Just say yes."

"Yes! *Sí!*" she exclaimed through her joy-filled laughter.

Julian lifted her off her feet and spun her around while happy applause rang around them. She felt her precious baby kick between their embraced bodies—as if the little one was applauding too.

Two years later

Cassie watched as Julian bent himself practically in two to try and fit into the miniature dollhouse he'd just put together. It had taken him a good two hours with no small amount of curse words that he'd tried valiantly to bite back for the sake of their small daughter. Not that little Julia would have picked up on any bad words she might hear. At fifteen months, she was much too young. She only had about four or five words in her vocabulary.

But Julian was the type of father who didn't take any chances when it came to his little girl.

And he was truly and undoubtedly her father. In every way that mattered.

He'd been present for her birth and had legally adopted her as soon as she'd arrived. Little Julia Rafael Santigo had her father completely enamored and he had been since the day she made her way into the world. Her middle name was an homage to her late grandfather.

Her aunties who worked on the resort as well as her paternal grandmother doted on her. And some resort guests who were already regulars, with several stays over the past eighteen months, could very well qualify as extended family. Her two uncles competed with each other to see who could spoil her the most whenever they visited. So far, the competition could be considered a draw.

Carlos, for his part, had remained technically true to his word about being a consistent presence in Julia's life. On the surface anyway. He'd shown up for her first birthday and called sporadically just to hear her babbling over the line for a few seconds. But as the saying went, a leopard didn't change its spots. And within a few months of Julia's birth, which he hadn't been in the country for, Carlos was back to his globe-hopping and fun-filled way of life. Still, to his credit, he regularly sent toys and other small gifts from the various corners of the world he happened to be treading at any given time.

Surprisingly, Cassie had received an email from Zara a few weeks back that she'd run into him in Portugal while Zara had been there for a photo shoot. Apparently, the two had gotten into a bit of a verbal scuffle when Cassie's friend had approached him to give him a piece of her mind. Zara would never forgive Carlos for the way he'd behaved regarding the pregnancy.

Cassie had tried to explain that it had all worked out in the end but it was no use. Zara would remain outraged on her behalf as the true, devoted friend that she was.

Cassie had long forgiven him. Looking at her daughter now, there was no doubt of it.

She had everything she could possibly have ever wanted. By all standards, her daughter was a happy and thriving baby with a charming and rambunctious little personality already developing. Her husband was a devoted father and loving, tender partner who still sent her pulse racing whenever he walked into the room.

Cassie hadn't thought she could be happier.

Until she'd woken up the other day with a familiar twinge in her belly that she recognized quite readily based on past experience. A quick test had confirmed her suspicions. She hadn't shared the news just yet.

Now Julian stood with what could only be described as a flourish and admired the completed dollhouse that had taken up so much of his time. To his clear chagrin, Julia had already lost interest and was across the room kicking at the large foam soccer ball one of her uncles had gifted her.

He plopped down next to Cassie on the sofa with a resigned sigh.

"I'm sure she'll come back to play with it at some point," Cassie reassured her comically dejected-looking husband.

"I don't know, *mi bella*. She's pretty enamored with that soccer ball. Has been since Guillermo showed up with it. He's determined to turn her into a football player like himself."

They both watched as Julia picked up the ball and lifted it over her head before tossing it into the air. "Looks like she may be a good candidate for keeper," Julian added, paternal pride clear in his voice.

Cassie bit down on her lip. She'd been waiting for the perfect time to make her announcement. Sitting next to her husband as they watched their precious little girl happily play in front of them, she knew it couldn't get much more perfect than this present moment.

She leaned into his side and rested her head on his shoulder. "Then perhaps the next *bebé* might appreciate the dollhouse a bit more."

Julian stopped breathing. Mouth agape, he took her gently by the shoulders to fully face him. "The next... Do you mean... Are you saying...?"

Cassie couldn't help her laughter as she nodded. "Yes. That's what I'm saying."

Before she could even brace herself for it,

he'd bolted up and lifted her into his arms, letting loose a flurry of Spanish words she only partially understood despite regular sessions with Maria.

But she didn't need to be fluent to interpret his absolute joy at the news.

"When? How?" he asked through a wide grin when he finally set her back on her feet.

"I just found out."

"Confirmed?"

She had to laugh at his repeated attempts at reassurance, almost as if he was afraid the news was too good to be true. "Yes. Confirmed. I have an initial appointment at the clinic next week."

"I'll clear my calendar. Cancel the trip to Barcelona."

She was about to tell him there was hardly any need to do that, but figured it would be a waste of time. Julian would insist on accompanying her.

The smile flattened. "How do you feel? Are you feeling tired or ill in any way?" The concern laced in his voice touched her deeply.

"I feel great, Julian. Like I have everything I could possibly want." Cassie didn't think she'd ever spoken truer words. The universe had handed her a life she would have never dared hoped for.

He responded with yet more Spanish. This time she fully understood even if she couldn't interpret every word he was saying.

Happiest and luckiest man...

Throwing her arms around his neck, Cassie met his lips with her own, responding in a way that needed no words at all.

* * * * *